AF416639

THE BITTERSWEET

VEIL OF ILLUSION

MICHAEL ALAN

This is a work of fiction. Names, characters, places, businesses, and incidents are either the products of the author's imagination or used in a fictitious manner. Any resemblance to actual persons, living or dead, or actual events is purely coincidental.

No portion of this book may be reproduced in any form without permission from the publisher, except as permitted by U.S. law. For permissions: contact the author.

Copyright © 2020 Michael Alan
All rights reserved.

TABLE OF CONTENTS

1: THE HIMALAYAS

Clouds hovered below, as we ascended the precipice. The outskirts of the village nestled in a distant peak, finally in view. Nantu and his yak wandered far ahead on the sinuous trail. As the curved passage narrowed, a cobra darted out from a crack in the ledge. Her poisoned fangs locked into my yak's leg. She cried out in agony and fell with all her weight on top of me as we tumbled over the edge. In a flash, alone and hanging by my fingertips, the peace and solitude of the Himalayans with the joyous anticipation of arriving at my destination disappeared; with a chilling realization, I am going to discoverer the portal of death I was looking for, but not in the way expected.

Far above the jagged crags below, dangling helplessly, and unable to lift my broken leg to get back on the ledge, terror took hold. In seconds, my life in its entirety passed before me, my country home, Rachel, the circus, and endless travels. What would become of Karin, now abandoned and my unspoken love for her? So many years and so little realized.

The moment my bleeding fingers let loose; I felt a vice-like grip around my wrists. The sun blinded his face as he pulled me up on the ledge. "Are you okay?" questioned the mysterious man. An unbearable pain paralyzed my voice, and everything blacked out.

With blurry vision, I awoke with a saintly face looking down at me. If I am dead and looking at Archangel Gabriel, I am in trouble, but felt an overwhelming sense of contentment. The aroma of strongly scented Turkish towels wrapped around my chest filled the heavily beamed room.

"He awoke from the coma just moments ago," the saintly man attending me remarked as Nantu opened the door.

"What magic did the Great Oswell use to escape imminent death? When your yak cried out, I turned and saw her falling into the abyss of the canyon, and ran down the rock-strewn ledge, almost slipping off the side. Crying with happiness and sadness, scarcely believing my eyes when I found you lying unconscious on the trail. I thought I would be picking you up in pieces in the abyss below. After immobilizing your leg, I tied you onto my yak."

We both turned, hearing a gentle tap on the stone wall. A stalwart man with large lustrous eyes looked down at us from the doorway. It must be the master, Okaala. "Well my distant visitor, I hope you are comfortable. How are you feeling?"

"A little groggy, I only feel a slight discomfort in my leg. Actually, I never felt such tranquility in my life."

"Don't get too absorbed in the 'loftiness' it will dissipate when the opium wears off."

"Oh," I replied, and felt as dim-witted as I must have appeared.

"The young monk treating you is very adept at healing; you

will be up and walking soon." As the monk adjusted the splinters of wood laced around my leg, I jolted back.

"Nantu told me you are the Great Oswell. Will you entertain us with some of your magic after your leg has healed?"

"I would be glad to, but I don't think it will impress you after all Nantu has told me about you."

"Well, Mr. Oswell."

"Please, just call me Oswell."

"As you please, what brings you to these lonely Himalayan heights?"

"At a Country Fair in New York, I met Nantu. He stood out in the crowd with his strange clothes and long braided hair. We stood next to each other looking at a fakir lying on a bed of razor-sharp nails. Nantu with a knowing smile laughed and said, 'I can do that.' Enquiring how the subject turned from physical powers to spiritual powers. He talked on and I listened to his stories spellbound. We became fast friends, and he traveled along with my circus. Not long afterward I received an invitation from a friend in Belgium to do shows in Europe. Nantu accompanied us.

"We traveled from country to country, but my magic tricks became tiresome for me and I felt a growing desire to do some real magic, something spectacular not just sleight of hand and abracadabra. Nantu talked often of the world beyond the portals of death, and the untold beauties waiting there. He also spoke of the Himalayan yogis and the supernatural powers over Nature they have.

"One day in Italy walking by a port in the Mediterranean, without a moment's forethought, Nantu told me, 'I am going home,' I knew I had to accompany him. That was several months ago."

"What exactly are you hoping to find here Oswell?"

"Knowledge."

"Knowledge or powers" questioned Okaala?

"Are not they both the same?"

"Power without knowledge can be devastating. Knowledge with no power can be useless. It is not only what you have, but how you use what you have. For what end do you want this knowledge?"

"To go to the world beyond and return."

"You want power over death?"

"No, not exactly, well yes, I want to do the greatest magic of all."

"Well, then I'm afraid you wasted an arduous journey, I do not teach circus tricks, but help those in their search for spiritual awakening. I'm sorry if you have been misled."

Okaala spoke no more and left. Bewildered, I could not understand his rejection. Having such impressive powers, I thought it would have been a simple matter for Okaala to teach me. Impressing others did not seem to be his forte. A good thing he lives here, I thought, for back home he would not be much of a success.

Soon I dozed off to sleep with the setting sun. In the morning I awoke feeling battered and bruised from head to foot. Drugged no more, cold hard reality returned to my being. The welcome aroma of food cooking on a wood stove entered the room. My stomach felt like weeks passed without eating. The young doctoring monk returned and mentioned, "After eating, you shall lie in the sun today and absorb her healing rays."

A short while later they carried me out to a veranda overlooking the vast mountains. Villagers sauntered by, going about their errands, occasionally giving a curious glance in my direction. One more deception, for I thought the villagers would be in awe to have an internationally renowned performer in their midst. A long arduous journey here for nothing. What a mistake I made. What a waste. Making the situation even worse from another room, I overheard Okaala reprimanding Nantu.

"Why did you bring Oswell here? He has neither a concept

of God nor a desire to know Him."

"Master, blind dogma is the only thing he knows."

"Then why didn't you try to enlighten him, Nantu."

"It just didn't seem right trying to impose my ideals on someone in a foreign land. I'm no saint."

"You don't have to be a saint to help someone. You are an excellent teacher. You enticed him with spectacular stories, albeit true, but not the essence behind them. He came for the wrong reason."

"But I was hoping this lofty environment would wake and arouse a spiritual desire in him."

"A heartfelt longing brings God to a devotee, not desires of fame. You know attaining the powers of the yogis is not some easy magic trick and doesn't come to one who covets power but comes as the natural blessings of one on the spiritual path."

"Could it be he came because of a subconscious longing to know God, yet masked by materialism, the only state he knows."

"Your quick wit does you well, Nantu, it has always been your savior. We shall see."

Early evening on the veranda I sat covered with woolen blankets; my clothes lost with the yak, scattered in the Himalayan winds. Two weeks passed without seeing Okaala again since our first encounter, my body was regaining its vigor. A gong with a deep resonance reverberated over and over in a not too distant temple, with a mesmerizing effect. "It's good to find you are doing well, Oswell. Do you enjoy the view overlooking the world?" Okaala questioned as he arrived unexpectedly with Nantu.

"It is indescribable, the feeling one has looking out at the vast sea of mountains; they seem alive with a life of their own. Can I ask you a question," abruptly changing the subject?

"Yes."

"Day after day I have been observing the villagers. Although they appear happy and quietly reserved, their eyes are unrevealing as though their thoughts are very distant, apparently oblivious to the surrounding tumult."

"They try to keep their mind on lofty thoughts, practicing the presence, while carrying on with their responsibilities."

"The presence of what, I queried?"

"God."

"Sorry, Okaala, but I don't need God."

"What does God signify for you, Oswell?"

"A handyman," with a little thought, I replied.

"A handyman! questioned Okaala?"

"Yes, my Lord they pray; please fix this, or I am ill please make me well, I need this, I need that and the other, and on and on. Then perchance if their prayer is fulfilled, the Lord remains neglected and abandoned, left by the wayside until their next need arises."

Okaala and Nantu sitting at my side gave a hearty laugh.

"Your objectivity is commendable, replied Okaala. But there is another way to imagine the Lord, as a friend and constant companion, as the villagers do. That is practicing the presence. It is the inner peace of the villagers you are confusing with absentmindedness."

"That is quite different from the precepts I have learned. I have not the vaguest idea of what God might look like."

"God appears in many forms to his devotees, to those of us here in the village He is Shiva, to you He maybe Jesus or Krishna or another great Master. It is only important that the form awakens devotion and the desire to reunite with Him in His blissful celestial grandeur. That is the whole key."

After an enlightening conversation, Okaala made one last comment, "One must be watchful of one's desires Oswell, for they can be deceptive and perilous for the unwary. They have the uncanny ability to obscure unexpected consequences on their journey to fulfillment. The only desire that will bring everlasting contentment is God. Eventually, all else without this one desire will deceive and fail you."

2: THE VISION

Later that evening, as I sat resting alone on the dark veranda sporadically lit by shafts of moonlight passing through the clouds, I felt the strange sensation of Okaala's presence nearby. Suddenly, I found myself transported instantly to heaven. Enticing and beautiful, everything I ever imagined, warm sun, lush vegetation, an absence of mosquitoes, and crawly things. Satisfied with the fruition of my long-sought wish, I walked along the edge of a gurgling stream, not even the song of a bird to disturb the peace. After a while, it seemed strange that I had not yet seen anyone. All remained silent, but oh so wonderful.

A chill ran down my spine as someone touched me on the shoulder from behind with the softness of a woman's touch. The sensual maidens of heaven, I thought, my heart beating fast in expectation of the pleasures that lie ahead. Turning around only to see the ugliest woman that could ever exist. She embraced me with the force of a bear. A distorted face and body covered with warts; she was a living nightmare. Letting out a scream, she hugged me tighter, her drooling lips pressed on my face. Suddenly she vanished, leaving me dazed.

On the grass, cute squirrel-like animals gathered around me. With a sigh of relief, I smiled and said, "Hello, my little friends." They smiled too, revealing mouths full of inch long dagger-like teeth. Now I knew why my maiden disappeared as I jumped in the stream. They stayed at the water's edge; I could only wonder why.

A single fast-moving wave began moving upstream towards me, I started running in the water and leaped up on an opportune boulder. The wave turned into frothing water around the rock. Okaala, "Help," I cried out, but no response. This is all just a nightmare I will just wake up, but I didn't and couldn't. Finally, a band of heavily haired barbarians came running my way. They put a log next to the rock that I could get to safety, or perhaps their next meal, while they kicked the waiting squirrels into the water. In seconds, nothing remained. They motioned for me to follow them when from out of the jungle growth came a fist-sized ball of light that hit and exploded one of the barbarians. They charged into the jungle.

Suddenly everything turned black, dead I thought. I awoke trembling in a cold sweat, but so happy to be alive. It all appeared so real. Not fair, I muttered to myself as I regained my composure; and went to Okaala with an indignant air about me.

"I did not choose your destination," he replied and spoke no more.

Again, he left me bewildered, I sought my dear friend Nantu and asked, "Where am I going wrong here? A broken leg and a living nightmare are the only things I have to show for this trip."

"Can I be open and honest with you?" questioned Nantu.

"You don't have to ask; you are one of my few faithful friends in this world."

"You came into a spiritual environment with your mind concentrated on ideas of material accomplishments, standing tall and proud amongst humble villagers; you distance yourself from them."

"Why doesn't anyone try to explain anything to me?"

"Have you asked?"

"No, where I came from, I am used to being educated without asking, as you probably well know."

"Oswell, what is it you want, recognition from spiritual powers or spiritual knowledge?"

"Both I had imagined."

"The two are in a way paradoxical. If you desire the knowledge of spiritual powers for recognition's sake they will not, as a rule, materialize. If you have spiritual powers and abuse them by not using the powers for the best possible good, you stagnate and eventually lose them."

Nantu, "Why didn't you tell me that before."

"I thought you came here looking for self-accomplishment. Nevertheless, you have realized your great desire."

"I don't understand."

"You wanted to go to the world beyond death and return. Okaala has granted your wish."

"Yeah, you're right. I never thought of that. But that's not how I wanted to go or where I wanted to go."

"As Okaala warned, 'That is the problem with desires, they rarely give the expected result. One almost always discovers something missing or unexpected.' But think of it, how many people do you know that have glimpsed the other side?

"You should have thanked Okaala, for his blessing you with that experience."

"Okaala must just shake his head in wonderment when he thinks of me."

"Oswell many in this world suffer terribly because of misguided perspective."

"What do you mean?"

"Can I tell you a brief story?"

"Yes, I have a little extra time today."

"That's good to know."

"Before I met you in New York I had been traveling for months across the States. I usually slept in the woods under the trees and ate the simplest of foods. Sometimes spending days with no food or water. Avoiding noisy public places and gatherings with the usual unholy vibrations. To me, the voice of silence speaks much clearer than the clatter of spoken words."

"Silence speaks?"

"In a meditative state of quietness, yes, intuition gives a much better understanding than words."

"The weather began warming up in March, so I started heading farther north. In early April I arrived in New York and wandered around the city. The following day a late unexpected blizzard arrived, and I needed to find shelter. All the hotels and Inns crowded beyond capacity, but I found a place to stay on Fifth Avenue. The owners of the large hotel were very congenial towards visitors like me who could not find or pay for a room but needed a place to stay. Filled wall to wall with people sitting or sleeping wherever one could find a space, smoking long cigars, drinking whiskey, and who knows what else. Others were already tipsy and singing discordant notes. The worldly vibrations were horrible, but I was very thankful to be out of the chilly wind and deep snow.

"The next morning, I awoke after sleeping on the cold floor. Looking at the mass of tired, forlorn people gathered there, I thought to myself, my traveling days are over, I have had enough. This place is the living end.

"At that instant, an Angel surrounded by a glowing aura appeared by my side and spoke with the sweetest voice, 'It all depends on your perspective.' I intuitively understood and had to agree. She gently touched my forehead and instantly I could see

God enshrined in every single soul that was there, myself included. He glowed with the light of the full moon. It was amazing.

"She then observed, 'See how concentrated God is here.' She gave a sweet smile and disappeared. The vision remained for days wherever I went. Day or night I could see Him in whoever passed by. It is still a blessing to this day.

"From that day on I lost my aversion to crowds and close contact with others. That is why I went to the Fair where I met you a week later."

"Do you still see Him?"

Circumventing an ego-centric reply, Nantu replied: "No limits exist to what one can do with deep concentration, will power, meditation, and His blessings."

"Does that mean He knows everything I do, and my thoughts?"

"Think about it."

"Nantu that can be embarrassing."

"Why do you think God gave the Ten Commandments to Moses? If we lived by them, there would be no embarrassing moments and we would have perfect inner peace. But not to worry, the great masters and saints say He is pure love mixed with infinite patience and understanding, and He knows how difficult it is living here.

"Even the past of many saints was not perfect. They became saints, showing us how to overcome our weaknesses and unite with God again by the example of their lives."

"Wait a minute Nantu, why does one have to unite with Him if He is already with us inside?"

"As a sunbeam of light makes thousands of sparkles on the ocean wavelets, the sunbeam makes the sparkles, but the sparkles are not the sun. It is the same with God. What we have inside is a microcosmic reflection of the macrocosmic; for beyond the cosmos and vibratory creation exists another aspect of

God, the transcendental Unmanifested. The Masters say that is our real home, endless ever new infinite bliss. To attain this and understand how is why yoga and meditation were given to mankind."

"Now I understand what Jesus meant when he said, *'Know ye not that ye are the temple of God, and the Spirit of God dwelleth in you?'* But I never realized that it was meant literally and not as a metaphor."

"Now what do I do?"

"I think Okaala is testing you to see who will win, the Great Oswell, or the humble spirit hidden within?"

3: HADES AND HEAVEN

"Good morning Oswell."

"Hello, Nantu."

"Tomorrow is Okaala's birthday and villagers will come from far away for the feast and celebration at the Temple. Okaala would like to see you perform magic tricks. What do you say? Can I tell him yes?"

"Okay, I will see what I can find to improvise a few tricks."

"Let me know if you need help."

The afternoon and evening I spent getting ideas together and looking for materials I could use.

The next day visitors began arriving early. Their arms were full of offerings for the Masters and God. In all my time here, I only saw the villagers eat the simplest of foods. But today tables were replete with savory dishes and sweets.

I later found out that they only celebrated Okaala's and Lord

Krishna's birthday. Lord Krishna was their true Master and Guru and considered Okaala their master in the sense of being their spiritual leader. The festive mood contagious, people chanting and playing mantras in the background. Mantras they told me are sacred sounds repeated silently or voiced in song, prayers, or in meditation to go to higher states of God-realization and or healing.

In the afternoon they all sat around Okaala, near the entrance to the Temple, meditating and listening to his discourse.

After an inspiring talk, he called for me to come forward. Hobbling up to the front with an improvised cane as he introduced me. While sitting on a large armless chair I motioned for two girls and an older boy in the crowd to come forward to help me. The magic received enthusiastic applause. Not knowing the reaction to expect, I was pleased.

When I finished my last trick, a boy around ten years old came forward and motioned for me to sit at a small nearby table. A noticeable subtle aura surrounded him. He did not speak, as he put my hands on top of the table, palms up. He then took a carved moonstone dragon about two inches square out of his pocket. He put it in my palm and then turned my other hand over it, like hands held in prayer. He then sat on the other side of the table, while my hands remained on top of the table enclosing the dragon. He sat still with his eyes half-closed. Several minutes passed, and he opened my hands. The dragon vanished. This was no trick. His shirt had no sleeves. The dragon dematerialized.

He looked at me and gave a slight bow with his head. He then stood up. There was no applause as the villagers bowed down to him as he stood. He returned their bow and quietly sat down amongst them.

I felt like a fool doing the tricks of a clown before the star of the show. Humiliated, my mind trembled in turmoil. Okaala sensing my resentment came over and quietly affirmed, "That is the greatest example of concentration and willpower. The ability came from many lives of devoted meditation. Atulya's destiny is to assume the role as the spiritual leader of our people. He did not intend to humiliate you. He would never do that. You will understand the deeper meaning someday."

Unconvinced, feeling that Okaala was just trying to ease my inner turmoil. Again, I end up looking like a fool in front of Okaala.

That evening after I stopped feeling sorry for myself, I finally realized what a miraculous event I had been a part of. A living example of the capabilities of man and that is what brought me here. Hearing a light knocking on the door, I opened it to discover Atulya. He did not say anything, he rarely spoke. He looked at me with his powerful eyes and handed me the moonstone dragon he used in the afternoon. He did not stay, but gave a smile of friendship, bowed, and left. Not yet understanding its significance, I put the treasured gift away. Invigorated by his visit, my heart felt relieved, and now knew what I needed to do.

Late at night, I began meditating at the temple when I would be alone; I wanted spiritual knowledge, and I knew no other alternative. Besides, I had nothing but time, and I could not do physical work in my condition. I found a translated copy of the Bhagavad-Gita in English and perused the pages over and over. Learning more about yoga and meditation, and little by little my understanding grew. I did not find meditation easy to do. I never realized how my mind stayed so full of aimless thoughts; difficult it was to remain still and concentrate.

After my vision, I constantly wondered if Hades existed. One evening a week later, while I meditated, Okaala entered the veranda and sat by my side. We looked at each other with a knowing understanding. He appeared pleased to see me making a sincere effort on the spiritual path. We sat in silence together.

Finally, he spoke, "Oswell look at the stars, they are vibrant, many with planets like our solar system teeming with life. Varied and countless with unfathomable mysteries. You can discover wonderful places, frightful places, and everything in-between. Just as in the astral cosmos beyond our material world you will find heavenly places and demonic places. Some very disagreeable places exist in the afterworld for those of evil inclinations, as you would now no doubt agree. Heavenly places also exist where the good and just receive their well-deserved bounty. It is all discovered as we travel back and forth between the astral and physical worlds, life by life in our upward evolution until we reunite with God in his boundless bliss in the unmanifested infinitude, where no negativity dares to enter and spoil the peace."

We continued meditating when suddenly; I felt a subtle sensation of traveling at an extreme velocity, I knew not if seconds or minutes passed, distance unfathomable. I found myself standing on a steep cobblestone road. The translucent beauty of the astral colors no one could ever describe. On my left were several tiny houses in a row alongside the road. Behind them, the terrain sloped leading to a wide tranquil river valley boarded by lush translucent green grass and meadows. On my right side stood a pine forest. The houses, more like huts, made of the simplest of materials just nailed up haphazardly, with no concern for stormy weather. On one house they adorned the outside walls with painted colored circles two feet in diameter, each one a different vibrant color, another house had wide diagonal multicolored stripes painted. The designs varied, but not the utter simplicity. The houses, the trees, everything made of light with a translucent radiance.

People sat here and there amongst the houses, deep in thought. As I passed, they would briefly glance up at me, so I know they could see me. The peace and tranquility overwhelmed me, even the rocks and trees exuded serenity.

As I neared a grassy clearing at the top of the hill, a group of people sat in a circle around a pleasant hoary bearded man, who wore an orange robe. They were neither young nor old but appeared as if ever youthful and vibrant. Whether my presence did not bother them, or they did not notice me I could not tell. Intuitively I understood as he spoke. The words were soft but in harsh contrast to the context of his talk.

"… The mutilated dead bodies scattered on the ground, their heads hanging in the branches above tied by their hair. The tribal wars were gruesome. Still, others caught and chained by slave traders. Far away in another continent, the winter lingered on long, cold, and deadly. The snow accumulated month after month, as the stored food ran low. According to the calendar, spring had arrived, but there was no end in sight for the winter. To the south of them, it was the end of summer, and the ground was dry, the vegetation burnt and wilted by the fiery sun. Hunger and thirst were taking their toll.

"Wars rage one after the other, soldiers killing each other, many times not even knowing why.

"They kill and eat animals without remorse. Doctors heal by cutting out diseased parts from their bodies with knives. Many times, they only have alcohol to drink for an anesthetic. People work long hours at tedious tasks just to survive."

"Stop Ran Baja a place so terrible cannot exist. It is not possible."

"You asked me what it was like in the age of Kali Yuga in the physical worlds. At times life is as though hellish there. A long time has passed, and you have put it all out of your mind. But mostly good exists even in that lower sphere."

"Why don't they just ask the Divine Presence for help?" One questioned.

"They don't see Him hiding in the flowers and resting in the mountains. People live under the hypnosis of Maya and the resulting restless confusion of their thoughts and desires many times breeds greed, misunderstandings, and an endless onslaught of difficulties.

"If all this was not enough, adding to their difficulties the subtle unknown presence of lower spirits many times influences the thoughts of those with a negative temperament. The lowly spirits from the Astral world are so subtle, one does not feel or notice their presence. But they can stir emotions and desires of all sorts in the unsuspecting, who usually end up suffering. Anger explodes, tempers flare, and afterward regrets, but the damage remains. And to make matters even worse, the fallen angel and his demonic cohorts have their insidious fun in that lower realm.

"But at the same time, God, saints, and the angels silently try to help and influence them on their journey up to the higher realms of peace and purity, where negative influences cannot enter. Spiritually advanced souls from higher planes also reincarnate there to help.

"It becomes a colossal tug of war for those working hard trying to overcome the endless difficulties and a way to find peace and happiness in their lives. This constant battle, and how to win it, so beautifully and graphically expounded in the Bhagavad-Gita. It is about an actual battle that took place thousands of years ago and how the inner tug of war we all face is in essence the same. The dialog between Bhagavan Krishna and Arjuna describes how with God and guru, courage, and a handful of one's inner warriors of good, you can destroy the armies of evil and one can reclaim his divine heritage of endless ever-new bliss.

"However, they are now entering a higher age, both technologically and spiritually. But, if spirituality does not keep a step ahead of the technological advancements, technology will become like an out of control locomotive, destroying all in its path, and breaking its promise of building a better world."

"Well, I never want to go there," interrupted another sitting nearby.

"You never know, they need our help too, Ran Baja replied.

We all fought the same battles and evolved from there or somewhere like it, as they will too. It is our schooling and how we develop true wisdom, mental prowess, mind power, and the ability to create and heal. Those of us living here have all been through it and completed our schooling.

"But we have plenty to do until we have finished all our lessons and we achieve the final goal of life, as Arjuna did, total union with God, which is to say, Yoga. Then the goal of life becomes fulfilled. The soul reclaims its omniscient, omnipresent, and omnipotent blissful state of being."

"Ran Baja, then what is the lofty sphere of the angels like?"

"It is a heavenly wonder of joy and indescribable peace. It is all vibrant transparency, but beyond and even more subtle, one finds the abode of the unmanifested Divine Essence. Another day we will discuss this."

"Sultana what are you going to do today?"

"I am going to the river valley to make flowers."

"And you Camina, what are your plans?"

"This is the date that my mother ascended long ago. I will meditate and invoke her presence, and talk with her, I miss her so much."

They all got up and went their ways.

Walking into the sylvan forest; you could feel the delicious aromas from the trees as well as smell them. Everything exuded an enchanting essence. With my eyes opened or closed, I could see. Later, returning to the road where I first entered, I looked to the river valley below, and to my astonishment instead of lush translucent green grass and meadows, one could only see beautiful flowers everywhere. When Sultana mentioned she was going to the river to make flowers, I imagined she would sit down and paint or draw some flowers. But no, she made an entire valley of living flowers. All the powers I ever dreamed of having were at her command.

With a blink of my eyes, the heavy sensation of my body returned. The newfound world disappeared. Later, when Okaala rose from his seat, I asked him, "Is this world really the netherworld?"

His frank response was, "Think about it." He remained quiet as he sauntered away.

His words hit me like an avalanche, feeling an icy chill throbbing in my body. Could it be I was a visitor from the underworld to that majestic land? Breathing heavily, I tried to regain my composure, but my mind was in turmoil.

4: ADIEUS NANTU

Nantu arrived at my door early, "Oswell come by the courtyard behind the temple this afternoon. I will be giving classes on the martial arts for the boys and girls and would like you to join us."

"Nantu you teach and encourage violence, and next to the temple?"

"The martial arts are self-defense and not aggressive. It is excellent training for the body and mind. When I was a boy at the monastery in China, the training was an integral part of monastic life. Alone, away from the protective walls of the monastery, one needed tough training and courage to survive. It teaches one to respect life, not abuse it. None of these children would ever aggressively use their physical abilities to harm even a spider unless it would harm someone. The training is not unspiritual. Come, it might surprise you."

"Nantu that's all very nice, but didn't Jesus Christ say, *'The meek shall inherit the earth.'*"

"Yes, he did. But he did not say the weak will inherit the earth. He was talking about humility. Weakness is not humbleness.

"Genuine humility requires strength and courage; mental, spiritual, and moral. That is what I teach them. Then one can be meek. Physical health and strength are an added blessing. The martial arts are unnecessary, it is just my way.

"For you will find the spiritual path is full of wonderful conquests and deceptions. Only the strong with a steady heart who confront life's challenges that test our forbearance, become meek, and attain emancipation."

Naturally, I went to see what it was all about. The martial arts were new to me. Sitting on a carved wooden bench in the roofed courtyard I watched in amazement the skill and agility of which they practiced their movements barefoot on the icy cold stone floor. They dueled with weapons I never saw before. Even wood poles became powerful weapons for them.

Thinking back, I remembered when traveling with the circus how Nantu with a slender build did things that only Eric the muscle-bound strongman of the circus could do. It was strange to see a man of such gentle demure with such strength and agility. Watching him, I finally understood how. His muscles appeared like flexible iron strands.

In my thoughts, I imagined how it would be to have them as part of the circus. Interrupting my momentary daydreaming, Nantu mentioned, "Some students listening to our conversation earlier got the idea of asking you to help them with their English. Would you like that? Many will go to college in India and it would help with their studies."

"Okay, I'll try it, but I have never taught before."

"Then tomorrow after lunch, let's all meet here."

After finishing their lengthy training session, they all went inside the temple. On entering they all bowed at the altar, which had a bronze statue of Shiva and a painting of Bhagavan

Krishna on the wall behind it. They meditated sitting on thick grass mats strewn around the floor.

The next day in the chilly afternoon the bright sun warmed the Temple and courtyard. Expecting to see a few boys and girls, I arrived surprised to find a large group waiting for me. I found them very receptive and enjoyed it all. We then planned a schedule until I would leave. Looking at the calendar, I silently reflected 1851 already; I will be thirty-five years old this year. It just was not possible. Thirty-five years old seemed so distant when I was a teenager.

One thing then led to another, and I became an active member of the community. The dreary months I feared turned into a memorable time for me.

Meditation, however, remained a tedious, uneventful effort. There were very few conversations with Okaala, but his words remained with me as a lifelong blessing. Wisely, in the beginning, he gave me wonderfully enlightening experiences as bait. And I became hooked. Getting ahead on the spiritual path had little prospect for the near future. Turning away and giving up appeared even bleaker. I harbored no intention of giving up.

November arrived with bright sunshine, and as I walked with Nantu he mentioned, "The harvest from the valley was bountiful and the food plentiful for the winter. If you want to stay on, you are welcome. I already discussed it with Okaala." Thanking Nantu for all he had done for me but felt it was my time to leave. Over a year and a half passed since I left home. Not mentioning to Nantu that although I knew their vegetarian diet was the right way, I still missed a lot of things like maple syrup and the smell of bacon frying in the morning.

Nantu then suggested, "It would be best to leave soon before any unexpected snow arrives." We embraced each other for a long time. I had little packing to do as I left all my magic equipment in Italy with my life long assistant Karin. Everything else lost on the climb here. Fortunately, I had my money tucked in my pocket when I fell by the cliff and could still pay my traveling expenses.

I sought Okaala for a last farewell. He greeted me with unusual warmth, "Okaala, how can I ever repay you for all you have done for me?"

"Show others the transforming power of meditation and the spiritual path."

"You want me to teach?"

"No, I want you to be an example."

"Okay, I will do my best. Okaala I have a question for you? Will I ever get to see something phenomenal?"

He looked at me quizzically, "The dragon wasn't enough for you? Oswell, have you ever watched a flower bloom? If one cannot appreciate a wonder like that, then no other miracle will satisfy."

"I understand what you are trying to say, but I mean like the stories Nantu always told me?"

"Well, now that you mention it, you already have. Think about the mysterious man that appeared out of nowhere to pull you up off the edge of the cliff, and afterward… nowhere to be found? It's a barren landscape over there."

"Did you pull me up when I fell over the cliff, I didn't see his face and Nantu didn't see anyone?"

Okaala did not answer, nor did his face give any revealing looks that he was just trying to be humble. Not answering my question, I took for his answer and thanked him.

For the second time, I bid farewell with Nantu and prayed we would meet again this life.

As we started the steep descent, I looked back towards the village nestled in the mountains and could see the distant peaks that blocked the harsh winds. Stone houses adorned every part of the picturesque valley. I then realized it was strange that no one ever mentioned the name of the village the whole time I spent there and questioned the guide. "He replied, Anahata, ascending the mountain it is the fourth village, and each village is named after a chakra. Anahata is the fourth of these spiritual centers going up the spine. One doesn't hear the name often because the villagers come to visit Okaala, not Anahata."

The descent was uneventful, except for a traumatic fear as we rounded the point where I had fallen. My legs were trembling so much that I had to pass that point crawling on my hands and knees.

We retraced the long arduous route coming here. The guide left me at the steamer that would take me downstream on the Brahmaputra River for the next 800 miles.

The steamer trip ended close to where the Brahmaputra enters the Ganges River. There I found a small boat that would go downstream towards the Bay of Bengal. Travelling along, the skipper pulled alongside the river's edge by the Taj Mahal. A magnificent architectural wonder, but its beauty blurred by my constant preoccupation with Karin; after leaving her so long, and alone in Italy.

The boat arrived at its destination, about 50 miles upstream from the Bay of Bengal. There I found a carriage that would take me down to the bay where I could board a ship for England. It would be several days of traveling.

The first night we stopped at a Tudor style Inn, near an English army outpost. Soaking in a long warm bath, something I had not had for a long time. As I relaxed there listening to the rowdy conversations coming from the eating hall below, the savory smell of bacon and sausage wafted in the air. I quickly dressed and entered the dining area. Travelers and English military men sat amongst the long wooden tables. My mouth watering after a long time of barley, dairy, and wheat; ambrosia my thoughts exclaimed. The first sausage entered my mouth, with a shocking realization that I could not swallow it. Did I really change, had Okaala worked such a great transformation in me?

Holding the sausage under the table, I quietly caught the attention of the innkeeper's dog lying nearby. The dog and I became fast friends while eating my fill of cheese, bread, and ghee.

Later in the evening, I returned to the dining hall where many of the guests gathered and sat conversing.

A traveler with a very unusual accent was relating his impressions of India with a saintly looking man called Satya. As I sat, the traveler Jonathan complained, "Everywhere I go here is full of snake charmers and phony mystics."

Satya replied, "God as the Divine Healer is the cure for all our problems, don't blame the whole for the few."

Jonathan turned to Satya with an indignant air and cynically asked, "As the Divine healer? Which one? How many gods do you have here, the street vendors are full of them? Conveniently, you have a god[1] for everything."

Satya just smiled and responded, "What you are seeing are representations of how God manifests in His myriad of forms that give structure to the Stars and the Cosmos beyond with all its intricate details"

Jonathan interrupted him and quipped, "But they are only statues that fall and break, where is the power in them?"

"The statues give form to the formless that people can relate to and call their own. These representations give humanity a means that they can begin a relationship with God.

"For in a search for God, most cannot conceive, at the outset, of God in his manifested state, let alone his unmanifested transcendental state beyond our vibratory world. God shows himself in such varied forms. The sweet softness of the Divine Mother. The exacting power of Shiva to renew the old, the suf-

---

[1] In this book: God spelled with an uppercase G is a devotional reference to our Creator, as well as other references to Him. Spelled with a minuscule g it is a general ambiguous reference to a god.

fering, and infuse life anew in them, as well as Divine incarnations like Krishna. Jonathan, do you believe in Jesus Christ and all that he preached and did?"

"Yes, I do."

"Aren't there beautiful statues of him?"

"Well, yes."

"Does that make him any less of an Avatar?"

"An Avatar?"

"Someone sent by God to help humanity."

"In his case, perhaps not."

"Would Jesus no longer be the great incarnation he was if you knew that he had an accident and broke his arm, or that he became ill?"

"A lot of double talk, I would like to meet one actual person who has seen this supposed god and all his abstract manifestations? Satya, I do not believe in what I don't see. Nor do I believe in Heaven and Hell and all the stories everyone tells."

Satya continued, "Can you be aware of something which does not exist?

"In denial of what cannot be; exists the concept of what it is, therefore, it has to be.

"For everything is that is not; otherwise you could not cognize it in thought."

The air remained silent as Jonathan tried to assimilate Satya's words.

But normality soon returned as he questioned, "Then why has no one seen him?"

"Jesus, Buddha, Sao Francisco, Muhammad, Krishna, Saint Teresa of Avila, Saint Francis, Moses, and many other saints and Avatars have seen Him, talked with Him, and passed His consul onto us, as well as many other unknown great ones throughout time. They gave you the way to God, have you followed it?"

"What way?"

"Jonathan, perhaps for you it is the Bible and the Ten Commandments. For many of us in India and those in the world practicing yoga, it is Yama-Niyama, the Vedas and the Bhagavad-Gita."

Jonathan's provocations did not stop, "Satya, tell me something. Why do these people around here keep singing the same thing over and over again? What are they singing about?"

"They are chanting to God."

"Well, then they must think god is stupid if they have to repeat everything to him."

"They are not trying to explain something to the Lord; they are doing this out of devotion. For various ends, they are repeating the same devotional songs or sounds, creating distinct vibratory states in themselves and around them. Many are mantras and just as some western music can affect the way you feel, making you happy or sad, these devotees use mantras to go to higher and higher states of consciousness and joyous devotion."

"Satya I will tell you, being a scientist at least we do useful work for mankind."

Satya agreed and continued, "In its essence science offers among many other things the dream of perfect physical comfort. But comfort does not come from fulfilling your endless physical desires, which leaves you exhausted and inwardly empty. No, comfort, genuine comfort comes from putting yourself in God's arms. That alone gives security, peace, and joy."

"Sorry Satya, but I only see poverty and suffering from all their spirituality here."

"Tests will always exist, and many suffer for the doings of others. But painful karma is not the result of spirituality, but the lack of it."

"Satya pick up a newspaper once and read it, and then tell me there is a God."

"Jonathan, sit with a saint once with the same receptivity you have for the newspaper, and then tell me there is no God."

"Well, you have answers for everything, but in the end, we will both be in the same boat."

"Perhaps Jonathan, perhaps."

Later in the evening as I laid down to sleep a bright glowing angelic figure appeared in my room, her translucent white garments flowing as though in a breeze. She was youthful and beautiful. It was just a glimpse, but overwhelming. I felt purified by the experience.

5: MASTER ZENKAI

I planned to take a ship around India to the Red Sea onto Cairo then cross the Mediterranean Sea to Italy where I left my magic equipment and other belongings with Karin. Then we would sail homewards to the States via England.

Before leaving, I bought pictures of Shiva and Krishna from a man selling them in a small shop on a nearby street. I also bought western style pants and shirts near the English army outpost. The only western style clothes I had was what I was wearing when I had my mountain accident. Since then I dressed like a Sherpa after losing the rest of my clothes when the yak fell of the cliff.

The following day I set out for the Bay of Bengal in a carriage accompanied by an English Colonel, his wife Lillian Blake, their daughter Gretchen, Colonel Blake's personal assistant George, and another young officer.

We conversed very little on this first day of travel. After dining together that evening, we all became more at ease with each other. The next day in the carriage we had a pleasant conversation, and the Colonel questioned me about my travels in India. Feeling at ease in their company, I spoke about my experiences in the Himalayas with Okaala. Traveling on as the miles passed, they attentively listened, I reflected in the background of my mind that I have found my true vocation in life with spirituality. The vision of the angel at the Inn could only have been a message that my life was to change.

Finally, Colonel Blake spoke, "Oswell you do not have to travel to the Himalayans to find saints, they are everywhere here. I don't need to practice meditation; I have already found god."

"You have?" Surprised, I asked.

"Yes, and I believe in him heart, mind, and soul."

"That's wonderful, Colonel."

"How did you do it? How did you find him?"

"By arduous work, Oswell, would you like me to present him to you?"

"You can?"

"Yes."

"Close your eyes." After a few moments he said, "Okay, you can open them now." In his outstretched hand, he held a gold coin in front of my face. "This is my god; he who sustains me, protects me, and gives me all I desire." They all began laughing uproariously, except me.

"Oh, don't be so distraught, my dear friend," remarked Colonel Blake.

In retaliation, I replied, "Look out the window at those poor suffering and impoverished people, they have nothing, nowhere to go and nowhere to turn. Do you know why?"

"No idea," the Colonel remarked dryly.

"Your gold was extracted from their veins." They all remained silent, as their faces turned somber. My first attempt to reform others I felt would be my last. The rest of the day's journey became awkward, and I decided when we stop for the night that I would remain there until the next carriage would pass by; and bite my tongue forevermore over spiritual subjects.

As I sat alone in the early evening, Lillian Blake came by and asked to speak with me. "Oswell I would like to apologize for our behavior today it was uncalled for. Will you accept an invitation to join us for supper? Your comment about the Indian people suffering because of our domination is a subject my husband has great difficulty to deal with. Because of his position, he cannot publicly voice his true feelings over the situation. Will you join us?"

"Yes," I replied. As we ate, the past tension dissolved in an amiable atmosphere. In two days, we would arrive at the coast. We relaxed the next day traveling, with the anticipation of boarding a ship and leaving the ever-bouncing carriage and rocky rutted roads behind.

The next evening my spiritual journey took a mystical turn. While I meditated a yogi appeared in my vision sitting in the lotus posture, his serious countenance accented by his long beard and knotted hair. Unlike the angel that left only a glimpse to remember, he remained and spoke. It was an intuitive understanding just like what happened with Ran Baja in my vision with Okaala. He told me, "It was time for me to help people. In my case, it was mainly to help them overcome fears."

"How," I questioned?

"When you meditate deeply, I will direct you. Tomorrow before you arrive at the ship tell Mrs. Blake that their daughter Gretchen will have an uncontrollable tantrum as they approach the pier and that she will not take one step above the water onto the gangplank."

"I don't understand."

"In her last life, Gretchen fell off a rowboat and drowned while playing with friends. She now has a yet unknown phobia with water. But do not tell this reason to Mrs. Blake about Sarah's past until later, when you are all on the ship. See if you can find a solution and resolve the dilemma first."

"Who are you?"

"Master Zenkai, the Tibetan master of the yogis," he responded as he disappeared. The next day when the coach stopped so we could prepare lunch, I waited for an opportune moment to speak to Mrs. Blake alone and told her that Gretchen would not enter the ship, not even go near the water. She gave me an incredulous look and replied, "Sarah doesn't have a fear of water."

Mrs. Blake, "Has Gretchen ever been near a large lake, pond, or river?"

She thought for a while and responded, "No, come to think of it. Gretchen was born here in India and this is the first time we are all traveling together. We have been through monsoons, but never to a lake or something like it."

Shortly thereafter she spoke with her disbelieving husband, but not wanting to cause disharmony again he remained silent.

We arrived at the port early afternoon. It was just a large pier. The ship would sail the following day. I suggested to the Blakes that they go to the waterfront to see Sarah's reaction when they try to walk up onto the pier. They hesitatingly agreed as we had nothing pressing to do.

A short while later they took Gretchen to the shore where the ship had anchored. As they slowly approached the pier and the crashing waves, Gretchen's serene face lit with terror as she ran off trembling. Shocked, they returned and sought me out. "What do we do?" I felt an untold joy and pride in my newly acquired mystical power and suggested, "Tomorrow morning let us take Sarah to a sandy spot on the shore, and see if we can turn water into a fun thing for her."

Early morning found us all at the shore. The gentle splash of the waves scattered the sunlight into thousands of tiny sparkling stars. Although she liked the sand, she kept a respectful distance from the water's edge. I found an old broken vase and started wetting the sand with water to build a sandcastle. We then built a second one closer to the sea. Finally, I sat by the water's edge as the breaking waves splashed me. Gretchen looked on curiously from a distance. However, when I got up and started walking into the water to take a swim, Gretchen's expression froze as she ran to her mother's side. She had enough. My purpose fulfilled; I would push the issue no further. We all sat and played a while longer in the sand, then returned to the Inn.

That night we boarded the ship with a little trepidation by the Blakes, but without incident to their relief. Gretchen slept soundly on Colonel Blake's shoulder as we entered the ship's cabin.

Seasickness from the heaving waves took its toll on us all the first day. Gretchen remained below deck, too sick to be scared. None of us ate that day. During the night, the sea calmed, and we all felt better and had a restful night's sleep. We found the creaking, smoky steam-ship devoid of amenities.

The following day's breakfast attested to the fact the ship's cook was not a fan of the culinary arts. As we sat Lillian Blake mentioned, "We would like to thank you for your help with Gretchen. Your insight has left a great impression on us, you possess unusual powers. Mr. Oswell, How did you know of Gretchen's fear?"

"Intuition, she has a phobia of drowning from a past life."

"I never believed in past lives and all that stuff. Well, not until now."

She then surprised me by saying, "I am curious about my past life too, can you tell me about it?"

"I'm not sure, it is not something I normally do, but I'll see what I can discover," I responded. Not mentioning that it was something I had never done."

In the evening meditating I sought master Zenkai. After a long wait, he appeared to my inner vision. Without asking he remarked, "Tell Lillian Blake that she had been Anastasia, one of Alexander the Great's wives." He faded out of my sight as I thanked him.

The next morning, I purposely delayed arriving for breakfast, as if I were unimpressed with the news I was bringing. "Well, Mr. Oswell?" With excited enthusiasm, Mrs. Blake stood as she waited for a response.

"Mrs. Blake," I began as she interrupted.

"Please call me Lillian."

"Lillian, yes, I discovered something."

"Well," she asked as all eyes were intent on me.

"You were Anastasia, the extraordinary wife of Alexander the Great."

"Anastasia, are you sure?"

"Absolutely."

Colonel Blake did not comment, as Lillian gleamed with contentment and pride. He quietly remained unconvinced of my revelation. Later in the morning, Colonel Blake sought me out, as I sat deep in thought near the helm looking out at the endless seascape. "Oswell your revelation to my wife impressed her deeply, but would you accept a test? Not that I do not believe in your integrity, it is just that I have only had deception in my experiences with horoscopes and fortune-tellers. I would like you to tell me something about my past and present tangible proof. Not as a curiosity seeker, but as a friend that would like to know that all this is possible. Would you accept?"

"What a challenge and understandable, I would ask the same of you if the tables were turned, I will see."

Again, I spent the evening in solitude waiting for a response from Zenkai. His form appeared in my meditation and it turned into a scene where the Huns had landed on the coast. Leading the battalion, I could see Colonel Blake; although slightly different in appearance, his long hair tucked under his horned helmet, it was unquestionably him. Engaging in a bloody battle, a swift sword thrust into his back left the Colonel helpless on the ground. Someone yelled go help Eric, I blinked, and the vision disappeared. Wow, do I have a story to tell. All night as I lay in bed sleepless, I could not think of anything else. Finally, I fell asleep at dawn and not waking until noon. In the morning, my absence unintentionally made the Colonel even more curious, and I liked it as if these grand revelations were an insignificant thing to me.

When I finally sat with the Blakes at lunch and told them of the Colonels past he again questioned, "How do I know this wonderful story is not just a fabrication of your imagination?" I thought of this during my sleepless night and risked it all on the probability that in many cases, as Nantu told me, sometimes we carry with us from one life to the next our pains and our problems and fears, and who knows what else.

"Well Colonel, do you suffer from a reoccurring unexplainable pain around your right kidney?" Lillian and the Colonel looked at each other with their mouths open.

Lillian finally spoke, "How did you know? No doctor has yet diagnosed the problem or found a cure."

"In his last life, at that point, a sword entered his lower back from behind in a battle he fought."

"Oswell, your amazing, absolutely amazing," replied the Colonel.

We did not discuss the subject further, and after lunch, I returned to my room where I stayed the rest of the afternoon until Lillian visited me. "Mr. Oswell here is a little gift of thanks for what you have done for us," as she handed me a small weighty sachet. Opening it, I found gold coins. She continued, "My husband can be very generous." She quickly left, expecting my rejection of her gift. Could it be that I could make money doing this, I wondered? Or is it unspiritual?

That evening I took my doubt to Zenkai and questioned him, "Is it unfitting to charge for helping people?"

"It depends on the situation and the motive. Your case is special, and your invaluable help is priceless. In one week, you have helped three people overcome problems. His entire life the Colonel worried he would die soon from what he thought was an incurable disease, his mind now at ease. Their daughter took the first step to overcome her phobia of water. Lillian living amongst nobility always felt inferior as the wife of a Colonel. You gave her a renewed sense of self-respect, albeit for the wrong reason. But no, you cannot charge for your help, your spiritual growth will stagnate. However, you can graciously accept gifts without asking."

Five days later we arrived in Colombo, Sri Lanka. The Colonel was full of ideas to bring me to England as a mystic. First, he wanted to enhance my appearance that I appear more mystical and bought for me a very dignified high collar black robe with fine gold lace trimmings, adorned by several jewels; even Merlin the magician would envy. The first time I wore it I felt awkward, but when the Colonel saw me wearing it, he called me "Swami, The Great Mystic" it all seemed to fit together nicely, the robe and the name Swami. He also suggested that I should let my beard grow long, which I did. I did not realize at the time that Swami was a monastic title with deep spiritual significance. I thought it just referred to anyone involved with mysticism.

We soon discovered our ship would not be heading for Egypt. Pirate attacks and slave traders fighting made the Red Sea too dangerous to pass. The captain changed his plans and would now go to Cape Town and let us board another ship there. Then we would go up the West African coast to Southampton, England. It changed all my plans too, not being able to go directly to the Mediterranean. Italy and Karin would just have to wait.

The Blakes did not hide their anticipation of arriving and presenting me to their noble friends. However, day after day the uneventful voyage seemed endless. The desire to travel overseas quenched, I resolved that once I arrived home, I would stay put on solid ground.

6: ENGLAND

What a welcome sight to see the city of Southampton, England coming into view. All aboard were celebrating. The Blake's invited me to stay at their nearby Salisbury home. In the meantime, we would spend two weeks here in Southampton. We registered in a quaint but stylish Inn in the center of town.

First, we went to visit their close friend Sir James. After listening to the Colonel's story of our travels, he looked at me with skeptical eyes, and behind his wrinkly eyebrows, I could sense the disbelief. The subject changed, and Sir James proved to be a cordial and likable fellow.

After the cool reception by Sir James of my supernatural powers, the Colonel put Swami, The Magnificent Mystic idea into check. The Colonel did not want to risk ridicule from his influential friends. As they left, Lady Caroline, the wife of Sir

James, invited us all to a party on the weekend.

The days passed quickly and Saturday night the Blakes and I left the Inn together. We arrived with a warm reception at Sir James's home. I felt out of place with England's refined nobility. However, they made me feel comfortable in their presence. They served rare wines with lavish abandon during the evening.

Sir James staggered over and in a loud alcohol slurred voice blurted, "Oh here is my fortune-teller. Oswell will you tell me, who was I in my last life, Genghis Khan or Caesar," as he stumbled around laughing. At that point, everyone in the room stopped to listen.

"No, replied Sir George standing nearby, you were Cleopatra." The smokey room filled with uproarious laughter.

I slipped out into the hallway that leads to the main dining room where most of the guests had gathered. Safe at last I thought until approached by Lady Margaret, a close friend of Mrs. Blake, who abruptly questioned me in front of a group of her friends, "I have a niece, Linda, who is very shy; will she ever marry?"

"It is difficult to find answers to these questions for I need time to concentrate on them."

"Oh, come on, she insisted, a question as simple as this."

As she spoke Zenkai appeared to me and said, "She is married to a young army officer."

"However, I continued, your niece is married to a young army officer."

"Dear Mr. Oswell, she is only fifteen years old and not married and probably never will be." No one mentioned anything more, as they all returned to their lively gossip.

Although embarrassed, Mrs. Blake tried to act as if nothing happened. She wanted to defend me but resisted the temptation, feeling it would only make matters worse. She earlier impressed Lady Margaret with stories of my powers. I just wanted to disappear from the party. I found a secluded bench outside and sat lamenting my coming and questioning what was happening to me.

Later as we rode home none of us spoke. The next day I tried to avoid the Blakes and stayed in my room until late afternoon. I decided not to go to Salisbury with the Blakes but would instead go to Italy to get Karin and my equipment and return to the States. In the afternoon, I headed down to the port to find a ship that was heading for the Mediterranean. Fortunately, I found a small ship going to Egypt that would first stop in Italy and made plans to leave on the following Wednesday.

In the early evening, I returned to the Inn. I just finished washing up when there was a knock at the door. It was Mrs. Blake, all smiles. "Oswell, I mean Swami, Lady Margaret came this afternoon while you were out and told me she received a message from her sister. Her daughter, Linda, ran off last Saturday and got married. Do you know to whom?"

"No," I hesitatingly answered.

"A young army officer; apparently behind her innocent eyes, lurked an alluring woman. Everyone thinks you are incredible. Here is an invitation to a luncheon tomorrow with them."

"Mrs. Blake, I decided to return to the States this week and cannot go to the luncheon with them tomorrow or visit your Salisbury home."

"Nonsense, if you don't want to go to Lady Margaret's home tomorrow that is fine, we can go directly to Salisbury. You will love it there."

I thought about it and realized I was only running away from embarrassment, which had now turned to pride. "Okay, then let us go to Salisbury, but I would prefer to avoid Lady Margaret and the chance of additional questions." Thinking that I did not want to push my luck with any new unanswerable questions. Now I could leave Southampton with my head held high.

The next day, before daylight, we headed for Salisbury. It was a tiresome day, and we arrived as the sun was setting. Their home was a large two-story country estate built in the Tudor style set in a grassy meadow. After three days of sightseeing and relaxing in the country air, Colonel Blake received a message requesting him to go at once to London. Sir James would come by Salisbury first, and then they would travel together. When Sir James arrived, he greeted me dryly, but that was expected. He mentioned that they would return in about a week, as they would only stay in London one day for the meeting.

The following day Mrs. Blake was moving a bulky chair and afterward complained that she pulled a muscle in her back and went upstairs to lie down and rest. She did not come down for lunch. Later in the afternoon, she asked me to bring her something light to eat.

When I left the tray at her bed stand, she asked me to please close the door as she did not want a draft on her back from the open window.

"Would you mind massaging my back for me?" she coyly asked. "No, I wouldn't mind." She stood up, slowly opened her robe, and let it fall to the floor revealing in its entirety her delicate pampered body. "Come here," she whispered, as I stood speechless not knowing what she wanted. "Come here," she repeated. Thoughts in my mind were racing in circles. As I approached her, I started to speak, but she put her finger on my lips, "Say nothing." As she gave me a light kiss on the forehead, someone knocked on the door.

"Mrs. Blake," hearing Private George's voice, Colonel Blake's carriage driver, she thought her husband had returned, and gave out a shriek. "Help, someone, Help me!" George forced open the door as I escaped with a thud jumping below from the bedroom window.

I only heard her say Os..., but not knowing what she told Private George, I could only assume that she accused me of the worst to save her skin. Taking a horse from the stable and grabbing my small travel bag, I rode as fast as I could for Southampton. Colonel Blake knew I already made plans to go to Italy and no doubt he would send troops searching for me at the port. On the way, I stopped at a village, cut my hair, and shaved my beard. Afterward, I found a horse stable outside of town and paid one of the boys to ride the horse back to the Blake's home, after letting her rest a few days.

Except for the clothes I wore, my money, and the things I had from India in my travel bag, everything else stayed behind.

7: KITTY VON KIRSCH

I arrived at the port late at night. Bobbies were mulling around with an eye on the freighter that I had made plans to go to Italy with. Waiting to find me and tie a noose around my neck. I backed off and lurked along in the shadows and saw another ship setting sails about to pull up anchor. Taking a chance, I paid a fisherman nearby to take me out on a rowboat. Climbing the rope ladder still hanging over the port side of the ship, I quietly pulled myself on board, hoping not to alarm anyone.

Suddenly, from behind me came a raspy delicate voice, "What are you hiding from?" Quickly I turned around and there stood a beautiful woman quietly scrutinizing me. She seemed misplaced on a cargo ship.

"Don't worry, I won't say anything. It will be nice to have some company on this long voyage."

"Come to my room nobody will look there."

Was she fearless, or leading me into a trap? I wondered if this was not a carefully orchestrated plot to capture me. To my relief, the boat slowly began drifting out to the high sea. Skeptical, but I kept quiet and followed her. Entering her cabin, she lit a lantern. Her flowing blond hair glowed in the mellow light. "I'm Kitty Von Kirsch and you are?"

I only mentioned, "Andrew Ellison," my first and middle name, I was not about to use the name Oswell again too soon.

"Where are you headed?" Kitty questioned.

"The States," I replied

"Well, I'm afraid you need a new travel agent, the ship is headed for Barbados. But don't worry, we will get you there somehow. I only have one bed so I hope you will be comfortable on the floor. Tomorrow I will get you a hammock, good night." As simple as that she went to sleep without a care who I was or what I was running from.

In just one day I went from a hero to a hunted criminal, but why? What was happening to my life, I was only trying to help? Exhausted and nervous sitting with my back against the door with the ship rolling side to side I was soon drowsy and nodding when Zenkai appeared and gave me a start.

"Are you angry with me? Would you like to meet Alexander the Great and his wife Anastasia?" Confused, I gave no reply.

He then held up both his hands in front, as he sat cross-legged, and in each hand, he held a large frog. Extending his left hand, he said, "This is my pet Alexander the Great." Then extending his right hand he said, "And this is Anastasia his wife."

He then metamorphosed from what seemed a sage with a fountain of spiritual knowledge to a terrifying demonic being; he came towards me and as he brushed by, every cell in my body iced over, it felt as though every drop of energy had been instantly sucked out of my being. As he let out a haunting diabolical laugh, I screamed, and his eyes turned burning red. His hideous laughter lingered on as he dissolved away. Dazed, I could only hope no one heard my screams.

The astral world never more for me. Never would I believe in spirits again, none of them. Shaken by the terrifying vision, and already mentally and physically exhausted, I lost consciousness.

We awoke by a knock on the door, "Miss Kirsch it is almost noontime would you like that I prepare breakfast or lunch?"

"I think breakfast will be fine, I'll just freshen up first. Oh, Pierre, make it for two. There is a guest with me that arrived at the last minute."

"Very well."

Cold and stiff after sleeping in a twisted position on the curved floor, I stretched my aching muscles a bit, the horrific vision still fresh in my mind.

The cook served us crepes with cinnamon and sugar, far from what I was expecting. I thanked Miss Kirsch for the hospitality. Obviously, the crew worked for her. Her delicate etiquette at the table seemed in contrast to her courageous manner she dealt with our surprise meeting last night, and I questioned her about it.

"Dear Mr. Ellison, if you want to play with beguiling eyes you need to learn the rules of how to play the game. Cheating is a challenge for them and the 'hapless victims' always scream for help when they get caught uptight and cozy. Good luck for the poor slobs that don't get away."

"How did you know?"

"Well-groomed and dressed men don't jump on to cargo ships in the middle of the night, risking who knows what out of curiosity. Just a feeling I had."

"I had nothing to do with it."

"No one ever does. Well, now you will want to know if I am married. The answer is no. My husband died three years ago, and I took over his importing business. So, relax, nobody will bother you here."

The afternoon I spent mulling around and getting to know the crew and talking with Kitty. But during the entire day, my unrelenting thoughts went back and forth trying to rationalize my situation and all that had happened. Wondering if God is inside us all, why does He let horrible things happen, especially when one is trying to do only good? Nothing made sense at all. What is the whole point of having God if he does nothing? He could have helped me and prevented all this mess. He knew I was being deceived. Who needs a silent spectator?

Becoming a hunted criminal; that is what I get for trying to move ahead spiritually. The only thing it has done for me is to open the door to hell. Well then, if we are already in Hades, it must be the door to hell's dungeon.

Later that evening I went down to Kitty's cabin and asked where I could find a hammock? She was lying down and in a soft voice replied, "Please close the door, I looked, but there are no extra ones. I found another pillow in the closet and put it over here for you. It is a little tight, but the bed has room for two." I froze.

"What are you waiting for?"

"I… I."

"Stop babbling."

"I'm married and she's a righteous woman; always reading the Bible."

"That's nice you know what she reads, but do you know what she thinks?"

"No, not really."

"With me, you do not know what I have read, but you know what I think. Do you have enjoyable conversations with her, like we did today?"

"No."

"Is she a wonderful cook?"

"More or less."

"Is she still waiting for you?"

How would it be if I returned home, and she wasn't there, and I passed up this moment? Never approached before by another woman and now twice in one week, two beautiful women want to be with me. I just couldn't think straight. Nothing made sense anymore. I found Kitty enchanting and sincere. She helped me with no questions asked when I needed it, I couldn't make her feel rejected.

"Is she attractive?"

My lowered eyes said it all.

"Andrew don't make me feel neglected, I'm very sensitive."

We spoke no more. That night she left me with warm memories for a lifetime.

But the next morning I awoke with a cold dose of remorse. The jumble of events left me so confused.

The following days came and went in welcomed tranquility. Captain Brinker took an around about route to try and avoid the windless doldrums in the Tropics. But even with all his experience, today we fell victim. The ocean and the air became still and quiet. We drifted at the mercy of the currents. The days passed, while the crew worked on fixing things that needed repairs. But now they too were resting.

8: HAHBU KAHN

That night Captain Brinker was in a storytelling mood and called us all by his side.

I don't believe in witches and abracadabra and all that rot. But I will tell you a true story I never told before. I just turned a lad nineteen years old, but already sailed the seven seas working on ships. We came from Boston after unloading a shipment of teas, spices, and golden laced tapestries from the Orient and dropped anchor in Mystic Seaport.

On leave, for a few days I was walking along a street shaded by oak trees whistling a tune, and when I came around a corner, I found a woman lying on the ground with a bloody cut on her forehead. She awoke as I lifted her. "Are you all right?" I questioned.

"I fainted," she remarked and paused, taking a few deep breaths. She then continued, "I came from that stairway over there and when I looked up all I could see were those ugly-dirty men hanging there swaying in the breeze in front of me."

"Then don't look again," I replied.

We walked away as I wiped the dried blood on her face. She mentioned her name was Daniela. We sat down on a bench as she told me the story of the hangings.

"Hahbu Kahn had been terrorizing the seven seas. With his bloodthirsty band of pirates, they captured the Conquistador, the most powerful ship afloat.

"It wasn't long ago when a fisherman returning to Martha's Vineyard saw the Conquistador at a distance. He knew the Conquistador well because a few years earlier on the high seas, Hahbu Kahn attacked the ship he worked on. A sword swiped his shoulder, and he fell overboard. They hacked the rest of the crew to pieces. The pirates ravaged his ship, then left. The fisherman then got back on board.

"When he saw the Conquistador near Martha's Vineyard, he noticed they changed the name to the New Bounty. Many of the crew were sick, and they needed supplies, so they risked coming here into port.

"The fisherman kept a quiet vigil after sending warnings to other fishermen on Long Island Sound. With small boats, they went out to watch as the Conquistador passed along. Finally, she anchored near Mystic a long way from shore not to attract attention. The militia quietly moved in and surrounded the city.

"That night Hahbu Kahn and his crew came ashore. The militia remained out of sight, for they did not know how many stayed on board and that ship has a lot of firepower. A warning went out to everyone, and the townspeople acted normally as though nothing unusual was happening. The pirates all went to Barnacle Bills to raise hell. There they treated captain Brimstone, an alias he used, and his crew like any other. The nervously smiling barmaids kept their mugs full of brew. They drank and partied all night till they all finally passed out drunk.

"The militia entered Barnacle Bills, shackled them, and then carried them off. Hahbu Kahn and his crew never knew what happened. The militia then chained them to a concrete wall, as the prison was not big enough.

"The weeks passed as the prosecutor presented a lengthy line of witnesses that came to accuse the pirates. Having no witnesses for the defense for their hideous crimes, hanging was the sentence for all of them.

"As he stood by the noose, 'Hahbu Kahn you are an evil man, repent while you still can.' He spat in the preacher's eye; indignation filled the crowd.

"As the henchman put the noose around Hahbu Kahn's neck he yelled out, 'You won't get rid of me so easily. From the portals of death, I will return, and hunt you down, and will kill you all!' His last words as the henchman left Hahbu Kahn swaying in the breeze."

Daniela stopped for a moment and questioned, "Do you believe dead people can come back?"

"Yeah, in the Orient where I have sailed many a time the people believe that we all come back eventually in a new life. They call it reintegration or reincarnation, something like that. But I think Hahbu Kahn meant coming back as a ghostly spirit to possess someone and do harm. He must have messed with the voodoos to know about all that."

Daniela continued, "At the courthouse, they stated that he was born in China to a family of wealthy merchants. He was highly intelligent and well-liked. For years he studied in the temples there. A brilliant boy turned evil. He looked for power from negative forces. Sailors say he is the devil in flesh and blood. Those that have seen him and lived to tell about it say his eyes are like fire, I could not look at him.

"It was Saturday night several weeks later; things were calm again in the city. A group of local youngsters snuck out onto the Conquistador drinking rum still stored onboard. Sarah Ann drank too much and passed out, and they put her in the captain's quarters to sleep. The rest of the bunch went home planning to return later that night for her.

"In the meantime, Barnacle Bills saloon was filled with drunken sailors. Captain Kialing, well known in the city, had passed out cold sleeping with his head on the table. Suddenly he jumped up and cried out, 'I'm back.' Then one by one his sleepy, drunken crew staggered out of the saloon, heading for the pier. They got in a rowboat and headed not to captain Kialing's ship, but for the Conquistador. In the night's darkness, unnoticed, they boarded her, pulled up anchor, and started raising the sails. Silently and slowly the Conquistador moved out of the seaport into Long Island Sound, heading for the high seas, with Sarah Ann still sleeping aboard.

"On the Conquistador, Hahbu Kahn, with his new body, entered the captain's quarters for the first time since setting sail. He opened the door and saw Sarah Ann sleeping on the bed. With a hearty cynical laugh, he exclaimed, 'Today is my lucky day, a princess for a present.' He picked her up and threw her on his shoulder. She awoke with a start. Kicking and screaming, Hahbu Kahn carried her up on deck. He tied her hands and hung her on a hook on the mainmast, her feet barely touching the deck, the crew looking on with hungry eyes."

Suddenly interrupting the captain's story from atop the lookout perch a sailor called out, "Winds off the horizon captain."

The crew jumped with a hurrah.

Captain Brinker ended his story without finishing and suggested, "Get some rest while you can, we will sail soon."

"Then what happened to her, the first mate questioned lightheartedly? If you don't tell me, I won't sleep tonight."

The captain called us close by his side. Then in his old English Pub style leaned forward and looked us all straight in the eye. Unheard by anyone Sarah Ann prayed and prayed a powerful incantation over and over again.

"By daybreak, the Conquistador reached the high seas and

strange clouds began to form, as the calm ocean began to rise and swell. Waves crashing over her deck with swift gusting winds. Pausing as he looked up to the stars…. For those of you who don't believe in a Higher Power up there, that protects and watches over us, I tell you true:

So is the spirit of Nature in all,
The ocean could not resist the heartfelt call.
The watery beast let loose
The sea began to brawl,
All hands to the deck was the desperate call.

The wind leaped on board
While the sea lashed out,
The mighty Conquistador was thrown about.

The main mast cracked, freeing Sarah Ann as it fell.
Too dizzy to stand,
Too scared to crawl
With a crash of a wave into the galley
Sarah Ann did fall.

Bite after hungry bite
The sea did fight,
With teeth slashing white.

With a final gulp, the last of the crew did pass.
Her belly full
She laid back to rest.

"The sea calmed. Sarah Ann remained unconscious in deep sleep after her fall. The Conquistador drifted on with broken masts, sails tattered. Weeks later the ship ran ashore by a tiny village in Shetland, now goodnight."

Mischievously the first mate questioned, "Oh that is so heart-breaking, as he feigned wiping his eyes, but what's the moral of the story Captain?"

"Miss Von Kirsch, would you be kind enough to give an explanation to this inquiring mind over here?"

"It would be my pleasure, Captain Brinker." With a look of mock severity, she replied, "Drinking and Sailing don't mix." They all burst out in laughter, rolling off their seats, except me. I did not understand what was so funny.

After saying goodnight, the first mate quipped, "That's the best yarn of a story I have heard in a longtime captain."

"Wait one moment," the cook called out.

We all turned around as a wonderful aroma wafted in the calm night air. Pierre had just come up from the galley with a basket of pastries. The flavor indescribable, they were pure ambrosia. How he did all his culinary work on this simple cargo ship amazed me. Serving gourmet food to the 'passenger' and crew, with entertainment; it was fitting that we were going to the Caribbean.

Later as we sat alone on the deck Kitty asked, "Do you believe all that stuff about spirits in the captains' story?"

"No," I replied, although I wanted to say yes.

She continued, "I do."

"Where I came from, they created an epidemic of fear about witches and possession in the past. Someone points a finger at a lonely spinster because of an unusual death or disease in the town, and before you know it, she is on trial for witchcraft. Then executed or held underwater to see if she survives. If she survives there is no doubt, she is a witch."

"What if she drowns?"

"No one is to blame. They are all just doing their righteous duty."

Kitty went below to her cabin. Alone, I sat wondering how I would ever get my life straightened out. I only saw insuperable walls in front of me in every direction. A wanted criminal, I reflected, and now an adulterer as well. What wonderful results the spiritual life brings. What was coming next, I wondered.

9: THE CARIBBEAN - BARBADOS

That night we all awoke with the first powerful gust of wind. The crew raised the sails, and we headed eastward to avoid any chance of getting caught again in the doldrums. We could have floated aimlessly for weeks. Now we were to take an even more roundabout route to Barbados. However, it would not be long before we would arrive at our destination.

Of all the Islands in the Caribbean, I ended up on a ship going to Barbados, an English colony. Day by day, my unspoken fears tied my stomach in knots. Could they be searching the incoming ships for a stowaway would-be rapist named Oswell? It is doubtful a ship could have arrived there before us with the news, but who could be sure. Then again, perchance nothing happened back in Salisbury, I needed to prepare for the worst. If caught I would be swaying in the breeze with my neck in a noose. One more story for Captain Brinker.

Sitting on some barrels with Kitty a day before we arrived in Barbados she mentioned, "When we arrive at the port, I will tell them you are Andrew Ellison my partner in my rum importing business." Now I understood why the crew found the remark about sailing and drinking so funny coming from her. Kitty continued, "You are from New York and I am from Nuremberg and we are working together." What a relief. But I still felt anxious, as the best-laid plans tend to go astray.

We arrived at the port and Kitty asked me to remain on the ship until she could find clothes for me to wear, for I came on board with what I wore and nothing more. The few shirts the crew lent me would convince no one we were business partners. Early that afternoon she returned, and we went to the Inn where we would stay for the night with no incident. Tomorrow we planned to travel north to the sugar farms.

Carefree and relaxed, a place where the islanders did not seem preoccupied with any of life's problems. The next day traveling along the west side of the small island we enjoyed a pleasing view of the ocean and countryside. We noted the English influence and their colonial touch, as leisurely days passed traveling around the island. Kitty told me that her husband died in a mountain accident in Switzerland; she then took over the helm of his lucrative rum and sugar importing business.

Although smiling outwardly, inwardly my subconscious fears ruined what could have been a wonderful adventure. I felt so at ease with Kitty from the first day meeting her. A beautiful woman, outwards stoic and straightforward, inwards warm and sensitive, the likes of which I have never met in all my travels.

We went to several unsophisticated distilleries, where Kitty introduced herself. She wanted to find new sources for sugar and rum. The owners lived in large estates adjacent to the sugar cane fields and convincing the owners to believe a woman was running an importing and shipping business took time. Kitty's charisma always to the forefront could disarm anyone. Together with my presence as her partner, it did not take long to make trusting business relationships.

After two weeks of traveling around the Island, she found and ordered enough barrels of rum and sugar to fill the ship. By the end of the month, it would all arrive at the port.

Barbados years earlier abandoned slavery. It gave dignity to Kitty's business knowing the sugar and rum were not the product of human suffering.

There was nothing more to do now except relax and enjoy the island. But I still suffered from the trauma of being a hunted criminal. Inner peace did not exist for me.

One day exploring the countryside, Kitty ordered the driver to stop our buggy by a ledge overlooking the transparent blue ocean. "Come, Andrew lets go down to the beach." The water was tepid warm. The offshore breeze was only a slight bit warmer. As she jumped into the water, the driver shouted, "Get out!" as he came running down the hill. Defiant she remained splashing around, the driver then blurted out, "This beach is full of poisonous spine fish and moray eels." She reluctantly obeyed and sunned herself on the white sands as I walked back up towards the road overlooking Kitty and the beach.

I rested on a smooth moss-covered boulder when a short while later a crumbly old lady came from nowhere, and without a word sat next to me. She stared down at her feet, embraced by the worn grass in the weedy field. She appeared forlorn, so without trepidation; I commented, "Why not look up to the heavens where God is." It just slipped out of my mouth.

She lifted her twisted neck and said to me, "What difference does it make if I look up to the heavens in the sky above, or the heavens inside?" A group of children running by brushed alongside me and broke my gaze as I watched them running after a large lizard. Seconds later, when I turned back to question her, the wise old lady mysteriously vanished.

As I sat reflecting on what just happened, an Angel appeared in my vision. The same one I saw in India. Oh no, not more of this and I closed my eyes. The horrors of Zenkai had finally lost their grip on my thoughts. But this time she did not disappear and spoke with a warm inner voice, "I came to warn you, but you subconsciously chose to see it as my heralding in the coming of Zenkai. Karma works that way sometimes."

She continued, "Performing astral abracadabra with startling revelations serve for nothing except ego balm. True visions come to those who have proven they know the value of enlightenment and the true purpose for which visions serve."

"But I helped the Colonel's family."

"He tricked you into this scheme when you were first given factual information. Then Zenkai mixed truth and lies."

"I thought to have Okaala as my master that he would watch over all I do, and everything would be perfect."

"The Master watches over and protects you, but you still need to do what is necessary to do conscientiously and intelligently. We get stronger learning from our errors, usually created by this 'inconvenient karma.' Okaala warned you the astral world can be deceptive and treacherous for the unwary. However, Okaala helped you by preventing Lillian Blake from turning on you."

"What do you mean?"

"When the Colonel's driver entered she quickly picked up her robe holding it loosely in front of her, scared of what her husband would do, she cried, 'Os…' and stopped in the middle of saying, Oswell." Then asked, "Where is my husband?"

"He is not here Mrs. Blake, what's wrong?"

"Oh, I thought I saw a face in the window. It was just the neighbor's cat on the ledge."

After her feigned recovery, Private George told her he returned after a half day's journey because Sir James mentioned to Colonel Blake, "That there never was a wife of Alexander the Great named Anastasia. Oswell is a phony."

She then asked, "How did he know about Lady Margaret's niece being married?"

"Sir James thinks someone told Oswell."

"And about my husband's back pains?"

"Colonel Blake believes he may have overheard a conversation with you both. He is just manipulating information his sharp ears are picking up."

"I'll ride back and let the Colonel know Oswell already packed up and left."

"Thank you so much private, you arrived at the right moment. That huge cat gave me such a scare. Please do not go yet I am still shaky. Why don't you get us both a drink?"

"She mentioned nothing about you, although she almost did. While you ran for it, she seduced the driver. Successfully, I might add, and that part without Okaala's help. That is why the army is not searching for you. Nobody knows you were in her room. Your suffering the fears of being a criminal have been unfounded."

Relived from a terrible weight, I now understood the horrible vision of Zenkai and the irony of his frogs. But the fear instantly returned as I thought, could this be one more well-planned scheme to trick me? There is no way to trust the astral world. How do I know she is not just another Zenkai? Reading my thoughts, she affirmed, "No, I am not one of them."

She then touched me on the forehead. An overwhelming blissful peace engulfed my being. I don't know how much time passed when she asserted, "Now that you have had a taste of what lies in the heart of higher states of consciousness, perhaps you will stop looking for miracles and reach for the blissful essence behind them."

Curious, I asked the angel her name, but she only replied, "Don't wait until after you die to find heavenly things. You will attain in the astral world that which you have reaped in this world, the good or the bad, nothing more. Only the blessings of God and Guru can alter this." She never mentioned her name and vanished.

It did not seem possible, but the nights with Kitty paled compared to the overwhelming peace she proffered. A touch of heaven, I wondered. Nothing like the heavenly idea I imagined of endless desires fulfilled with maidens and glorious delights. The angel's touch gave me something subtle, unexplainable in earthly terms, something joyous, all fulfilling, earthly pleasures paled in comparison. I now knew that I had to do everything possible to discover for myself what else lies in this subtle, but magnificent world beyond. Different from the visions I saw when I meditated in the Himalayas, but each with its enlightening aspect.

Light-hearted, I walked back down to the beach and sat by Kitty. The vibrant scenery awoke with a new liveliness. We walked along the water's edge for miles, kicking and splashing along the way. Back at the carriage, we decided this is where we will retire. We would build a home here on this very hill in the middle of paradise. The following days passed in tranquil oblivion, roaming about.

Barrels of rum and sacks of sugar began arriving at the ship. We inquired at the dock when I could get a ship going to America. They told us that although there is no way to know exactly; they come by often, it would be no problem.

Kitty decided she would go to New York after unloading the ship in Europe. She would arrive near the end of winter. I gave her my address and an address in New York where she could stay and get in touch with me. The people knew where I lived. When I arrive home, I would discuss separation with my wife Rachel.

Three days before Kitty planned to set sail, she awoke with terrible pains in her stomach, and I summoned a doctor. After examining her, he commented that it was nothing serious and would pass. He gave her herbs for tea and told her to drink coconut milk every day for her liver. The departing day arrived and by the evening she was well again, and they set sail, leaving me behind. I felt lost, but I looked with great expectations for the future.

Daily I went to the docks as the days passed by, then weeks and no sign of a ship. Worried, I started questioning again those working around the dock and the fisherman. Their answer always was, soon and sure enough, the next day a ship arrived. I talked to the captain, and he said the ship was going back to South Africa. Walking by were two sailors that had arrived with the same ship, and I asked them if they knew when there would be a ship going to the States and they replied, "probably never."

"But they told me ships are always going to America." They acknowledged, "Yes, there are many that go to South America and sometimes Panama, but not North America. From here I doubt any ship will head there soon. You are better off finding a ship going to Europe. A mail ship from England should come soon. You can go back to England on it. Then find a ship heading for Boston or New York." Being stuck and alone, Barbados turned into something less than paradise. I thought of other possibilities.

I inquired about smaller boats going to other Islands northwest of Barbados. But I quickly realized island hopping could be even more difficult and dangerous. I should have gone back with Kitty and taken a ship from Europe.

Weeks passed, and depression started taking hold as the hope of getting out dwindled by the day. The gold coins that Mrs. Blake had given me as a gift, were a blessing of security for me now. So far, I only spent money on the trip from India to England and the inexpensive lodging here.

One week later, early morning a wonderful surprise as I walked towards the shore and looked out to the sea; there sat a British Ship anchored close to the docks. A chance to get back to England, I could only hope the angel told me the truth; that I was not a wanted criminal.

Arriving at the dock I asked the sailors mulling around about the ship's destination and to my surprise and relief they replied, "Norfolk, Virginia." My elation did not last long, as they informed me that no civilians can board a military vessel. However, I entertained no thoughts of passing up this opportunity. I found a few decks of playing cards in the afternoon. They were crude and worn, but they would do. Later at night, I joined them when they were free to party it up.

During the evening, before they were too drunk, I beguiled them with my sleight-of-hand tricks. Receiving hearty applause, I felt wonderful doing something that I did well again. We all became friends and the following day after a lot of conversation I received an invitation to join them on the trip to Norfolk. The captain proved to be a very reasonable fellow.

It was a double dose of happiness: I was returning home, and the realization that doing magic was still what I most enjoyed.

10: HOMEWARD BOUND

Onboard high stacks of crates crowded the deck. The ship came to Barbados to deliver supplies and get fresh water. They were now heading to Virginia delivering sealed cargo for the government. They would not stop along the way at the other Islands.

I spent my free time working out new sleight-of-hand magic that I could perform. Doing magic again was not the tedium I feared. But fun and knowing I could help people forget their difficulties for a moment. Once I get back home, I decided, the circus would get going again. It took a heavyweight off my shoulders knowing what I would do.

The days passed quickly, and soon we would arrive in Norfolk. In the background of my mind, the harbinger of wintry cold thoughts of my returning home to my wife, Rachel, chilled the warm summer memories of Kitty. It was like a dream bubble that could burst.

We escaped the hurricanes and tropical storms the crew had feared and entered the Chesapeake Bay. They planned to make

their delivery and get out as fast as they could as they were behind schedule getting to Boston. Just a matter of minutes after
arriving in Norfolk, the crew began unloading the cargo and
bringing other crates aboard.

After farewells and promises to meet again, I went ashore. I
bought a ticket on a carriage heading for Richmond, Virginia.
From there I would take the railroad to New York, then a short
trip to my Connecticut home nearby.

In New York, I planned to stay a few days and look up my
old circus crew and see how we could get a show together again.
Also hoping Karin had somehow managed to get back from
Italy. The sparkle of the show, and without her, I do not know
what I would do.

This was only the second time I traveled by train. Our cara-
van always traveled by our horse-pulled wagons. The speed and
ease of going by train amazed me. New advances in science
mystified and scared people.

After a relaxing trip to New York City, the piercing whistle
sounded as the train screeched to a stop ending a whirlwind of
two years of travels. With a deep breath, I descended to the
platform packed with travelers, and others waiting for friends
and relatives. Weaning my way through the crowd, I then took
a carriage to the West Side.

Arriving, it appeared more decrepit than I remembered.
Searching for my tent handler, Johnny, I found him in an old
run-down shack. He had been out of work since I left. He found
it almost impossible to find new circus work living there. We
reminisced for hours and finally made plans to get together the
next day with B Bob the clown and others from the circus at
our favorite drinking spot.

I found a room to stay for the night before wandering about
the city. We all met the next day. It was so nice to get together
with my old circus friends, as I sat with the first beer in my hand
since traveling with Nantu. We lived wonderful times together,

and challenging times. I felt reunited with my family again. Life was getting back to normal for me, and I felt so good, relieved of all my recent stress.

With my first beer in hand, the others were on their fourth. The rowdiness of the place and the off-color comments I found repulsive, but I hid my inner thoughts and could not wait to be alone again. What transformation took place in my life, I silently wondered? At the end of the evening, we promised to get together as soon as possible to get on the road again. But doubts were assailing my subconscious. Now what?

The path to divine awakening seemed more like a never-ending downhill slide into oblivion, while the spiritual heights eluded me. The quiet Okaala, I mused, an artist in the transformation of souls. Slowly my understanding grew of the quiescent power that flows over the planet from these great embodiments of spirit, unknown, unpretentious guardians of the world.

At daybreak, I avoided the train and went home by carriage. A light snow covered the bare trees. A beautiful view, but after being in the tropics I wondered why anyone would live in the cold north. Well, at least I would return to a warm fireplace and home cooking.

What a welcome sight, my country homestead. After paying the driver, I went up the walk. To my surprise, I found no sign of Rachel or our dog. The house had a fresh woody scent, but the cabinets were bare. No food and no wood for the fireplace.

My good neighbors Sam Johnson and his wife Ingrid soon appeared and mentioned that they were taking care of my horses and invited me for dinner. While trying to get a hint about Rachel's whereabouts, I talked nonchalantly of my travels. The only thing they knew was that Rachel went to her mother's home in New York. Before leaving, Ingrid invited me to come every day to eat dinner with them until Rachel returned. I thanked her and accepted her offer as cooking was not my specialty.

The following days I chopped and split wood to pass the time and warm the house. A winter of solitude began. Daily I walked to the general store to buy things and meet old friends.

Today I went to the bank to put the gold coins that the Blakes gave me in a safe deposit box and see how much interest I earned on my savings account. The clerk looked up my account and informed me, "The interest accumulated amounts to 25 cents."

"25 cents, it must be a mistake," I remarked.

"No mistake. The $10.00 yields 25 cents interest."

"But I have over five thousand dollars in my account."

"Mr. Oswell, Rachel withdrew everything except the ten dollars six months ago. She must have mentioned it to you."

"No, I just arrived from doing shows overseas. Rachel is at her mother's house in New York.

"How much is this gold worth?"

After testing and calculating, the clerk replied, "$289.00."

Well, I still had money from my travels to live on for a while. How am I going to put a circus together with no money? Well, I thought, she just moved the money to a bank closer to her mother's home. Anyway, knowing Kitty would arrive within a few months left my mind at ease with the situation.

Although I had nothing to distract me, every night I made plans to sit and meditate, and something always interfered. I made plans to do even more the next night, day after day. Finally, when I meditated, my mind had other ideas and jumped from one thought to another; what I should have done, what I would do, and thoughts about everything except what I intended. The heavenly bliss I awaited seemed all too distant, all too impossible; my determination came in spurts, but I never gave up.

In the brisk night air, sitting on the sprawling veranda one late afternoon reminiscing, I recalled Rachel's repeated insistence on building a large Victorian-style house here in front. I always listened intently. But as the sun set behind the distant hills, I felt a warm sensation of peace as racoons sauntered up the steps for their evening treat in our rustic home.

Birds flew into the rafters, while two fawns played by the brooks edge. Their mother and father wandered off by the two-story circus barn, while nonchalantly walking alongside the horses in the stable.

The performers and workers all stayed in the guest house when we were getting the show ready to travel. It all served our needs well.

I felt content that her building plans never materialized as I went inside to stoke up the wood stove that kept the inside warm and cozy in the winter.

The uneventful winter gave way to spring with no sign of Karin, Rachel, or Kitty. Kitty's question if I were sure Rachel would be here waiting for me percolated in the background of my mind. Did she have such far-reaching intuition? But where was Kitty? Did she already go to New York and not find anyone at the address I gave her? But then again, she knew my address here. She would have come, maybe she found someone else, and will never come. Either way, I would make no new plans with a circus until I knew for sure about Kitty and what Rachel did with our savings.

The days warmed and remained pleasant, and I went to New York to the home of Rachel's mother. A lively woman with a friendly nature about her. She welcomed me with open arms as always. As far as she knew Rachel's sister Carol had a severe illness and Rachel is living with her and taking care of her. But she had not seen either for over a year and a half now. Carol lived upstate in Albany and had moved since the last time she saw her. She mentioned that she would get word to me about Rachel as soon as she found the address or when one of them visited again.

I found my life at home at a total standstill, spiritually, mentally, and physically. Month after month I had nowhere to go and nothing to do. Karin never arrived back from Italy and I worried constantly about her, not knowing if she was in trouble or had problems. And Kitty still had not shown up either. If Karin did not return by the middle of August, I decided I would leave for Italy. I would need to sell a few of the horses or borrow the money until Rachel returned with our money. I would have left already, but then what would happen if Kitty arrived while I traveled. Day by day my mind went back and forth trying to resolve an irresolvable dilemma.

11: TRIPLE TROUBLE

A week after August arrived with a heatwave, I heard a carriage coming up the drive. It must be Kitty as I ran to the door with the excitement of a teenager only to find Rachel. Her frosty coolness gave no relief to the summer heat.

She complained endlessly about my travels and deserting her and spoke of the dire need her sister has for money to pay for doctors and medicine.

"Where is the money from the bank account? There was enough there to build a new home and with plenty of extra land and anything else we might have needed."

Rachel retorted, "The bills were endless, and I need more money."

Disbelieving I had no money, she went on a rampage, calling me a worthless idiot, a useless fool, and on and on. Coming here hoping I earned lots of money in Europe and brought it all back with me; she became distressed to find I did not have any.

Our neighbors Sam and Ingrid Johnson hearing the commotion stopped by. A Blessing for me as Rachel turned into a picture of sweet loveliness.

"Welcome, I missed you both so much, how are you?" Rachel asked. Fortunately, the rest of the day we spent in their company. Rachel never mentioned if she planned to stay or would return to Albany, and I did not ask.

Late the next morning I heard another carriage coming up the drive. That must be her sister, I thought, to come and live with us. I did not get up to see; the situation getting worse by the minute. Rachel had walked out to the garden in the back by the brook. After several knocks on the door, reluctantly I got up and opened it. To my disbelieving eyes, Kitty Von Kirsch was standing there, more beautiful than ever.

"Hello, Andrew."

At that point, Rachel entered the back door and stood with her mouth gaping.

"Hi, Kitty." She did not advance to hug me.

"I'm so glad you are here, Andrew, I brought something for you." She walked back to the carriage and took out an enormous basket, I could only imagine what kind of exotic present she must have brought from one of her travels.

Walking back up to the doorway she said, "Here take this basket it belongs to you." She removed the blanket, and I became lightheaded and short of breath and almost fell. "She is why I was getting sick every day before leaving Barbados and it didn't stop until I arrived home. It was a horrible voyage." My heart pounding so fast I could not speak as she returned to the carriage and brought two more baskets.

"What are you waiting for? Pick her up, she is yours." Kitty remarked, "I don't have time to take care of a baby, I have a business to run and employees to watch after. The baskets have all the things you will need for her. You can do a much better job than me raising a child."

As simple as that she started walking back to the carriage. Turning her head, she continued, "Her name is Karina. Goodbye Andrew, I will always remember the wonderful time we had together."

Before I could turn around, Rachel's fists were pummeling me. "You horrible dirty man, I have been married to an adulterer," she cried. Her fists did not stop, nor her barrage of obscene language, my head reeling. Nightmares nonstop in my life, my thoughts in turmoil. What am I going to do now? Nothing could be worse. I was so dazed I neither heard Rachel's screaming or the baby crying, not even another carriage that pulled up to the door.

I turned around as someone else began beating me from behind. Rachel finally stopped to stare. Karin had arrived and took over the pummeling and verbal barrage. Finally, hearing the baby crying, Karin stopped and went over to the basket.

She picked up the baby and held her firmly on her comforting breasts. The baby stopped crying that very instant. One of the baby's tiny hands reached out and tightly grasped Karin's long silky blond hair.

"Whose baby is this?" she questioned.

"It's his," retorted Rachel.

"I'm leaving, you bastard, you haven't heard the end of me." She picked up her bag and got in the carriage that Karin came in and left.

"With the baby in Karin's arms, I finally felt safe. We were both panting. She wanted to say so much so fast she choked on the words. Taking a deep breath, she finally asked, "Is this baby yours?"

"I'm not sure."

"How can you not be sure? Is she, or isn't she?" Lifting the baby from her breast and looking at her face for the first time Karin remarked, "She's beautiful, what is her name?"

"Karina, I think she was named after you."

"After me, by whom?"

Relating the tumultuous events that passed since I last saw her, the hours passed and she seemed to be in an understanding, almost forgiving mood. I then asked her how she managed to get back.

"I waited for you and cried, waited, and cried. All alone and depressed in a foreign country, it was the worst time of my life. Finally giving up waiting for you, I found a fisherman who was going to England with his crew, and he let me go along on the trip. I had to leave the show equipment behind.

The steamship was too expensive, so I went by sailboat, and it took three times as long to get here. I had just enough money left to pay for the passage and to get here."

"I will send a letter to Raffino to pick up the magic equipment when his circus goes there, or to send somebody to pick it up. He can keep it all, after all the favors he did for us traveling with him."

"Somehow, I wish I could have contacted him, but he is always traveling, lamented Karin."

I then took advantage of the opportune situation to say something I never dared to say before. "When I was at death's door hanging off the ledge in the Himalayas and my life flashed before me do you know what I most regretted?"

"No, how could I?"

"All those years never telling you how much I loved you."

"You love me?"

"More than you will ever imagine."

"Why didn't you ever say anything?"

"I could not, I had a wife and feared I would scare you off. I could not do the show without you."

"Andrew you fool, I cannot believe what you are saying."

"Are you angry?"

"Andrew when I started working for you fifteen years ago as a young girl you took me in and became a father and brother to me, although you weren't much older. As I grew up, many a night before falling asleep I fantasized you and I were married and how wonderful our life was together. Year after year I lived traveling with the show all smiles with bleak inner loneliness, never a boyfriend or someone to give me warm affection. I prayed and prayed to have someone of my own, but God never answered. My faith faded and faded until finally in Italy my faith in God ended for good. Maybe I was wrong?"

She wrapped Karina in a blanket then walked over to me and embraced me and I just melted in her warmth. So many years I waited for her to hold me in her arms. For the first time, I tasted love; I savored the moment like none other. It was so different from what I thought I had for Kitty. It did not last too long as Karina woke up crying.

"She must be hungry," Karin mentioned as she held her gaze for a long time looking straight in my eyes, slowly releasing her grip. She picked Karina up and put her to her breast to feed.

"Karin you have no milk, she needs to eat something."

"Yes, I know, but I remember when I was a child, a neighbor of ours adopted a tiny infant and after a week, she had milk. Everyone thought it impossible. I will just let her suckle a few minutes. We can make some porridge for her."

Karin and Karina spent the night nestled together. They both looked the picture of contentment together. Karina slept soundly, but I do not think Karin slept at all. In the morning I quietly slipped out of bed and put wood in the stove to make coffee and boil water for the porridge. I sat back and wondered what I would have done with the baby without Karin. It could only have been Divine intercession. No other explanation would suffice.

Karin soon woke up, then came over and lightly caressed my head with a gentle touch.

"Good morning mom. Did you sleep well?"

"I fell asleep only after you got up."

"You must be exhausted after a sleepless night and traveling all day yesterday."

"I never felt better in my life. I guess we will all eat porridge again. Can we go to the general store and buy some supplies today?"

"Whatever you wish."

While she made breakfast, I started unpacking the baskets and putting away the things Kitty brought for Karina. Noticing a large envelope tucked between two blankets, I opened it and found a note:

Dear Andrew,

I do love you. Our time together will always bring beautiful memories to me. But it is in the past and I am content to know that you will be an exemplary father for Karina, much better than I could be a mother. I hope the money I am leaving you will somehow compensate. It should be enough to take care of all her needs.

Yours truly, Kitty

I carefully unwrapped the packet and inside found $10,000.00. A small fortune, and the second dose of divine intercession. She must have given me all she earned from her shipment. It would not end up in the same bank account, I would find a safer place, as no doubt Rachel would divorce me and politely ask me for every cent I have.

Later that day at the general store we received questionable looks from those who knew us. I found it an effortless task to read the thoughts on their minds. Billy an old-time friend and the owner could not wait any longer and blurted out, "Whose baby is it?"

"That is Karina. You remember Karin, don't you?"

"Of course, I do, you don't see too many southern bells the likes of her in these parts." Audaciously he then questioned, "And Mrs. Oswell, where is she?"

"She is taking care of her sister up in Albany."

"Oh, now I understand." But he did not, and it left him confused, which is all I wanted. My comments took the pressure off trying to explain where the baby came from and put an end to the interrogation. The gossip that would start because of Karina had fuel, but nothing to light it with. Karin only smiled and kept busy picking up the dry goods and other things she needed.

12: KARINA

Steadfastly before every meal, Karin continued in her attempt to breastfeed Karina, but they still offered no nourishment. We just finished eating breakfast when Sam and Ingrid Johnson knocked on the door. They returned from a brief trip and were overly anxious to see firsthand the situation with me and Rachel, only to find Karin and Karina with me. They knew Karin well from her past stays at my house during breaks from our circus travels.

Karin made them coffee. Forgetting about Rachel after a bit of light gossip, Ingrid unceremoniously questioned, "Who is the father?" I was in the kitchen when I heard the question and I choked on my coffee as the cup fell clanging along the floor.

"Are you all right?" Karin quizzically questioned with an ironic air.

"Yes, I'm fine, a wet cup slipped out of my hand."

Karin mischievously continued, "Oh I'm sorry Ingrid, what

did you just ask me?"

"Who is the father?"

"Never I have met a more wonderful man. Intelligent, polite, conscientious, and handsome he...." An opportune whimper from Karina put an end to the conversation as Karin excused herself saying, "She must be hungry." The Johnsons soon left content, but as confused as Billy at the general store.

Later in the evening, we talked about the money that Kitty left and decided to keep it well protected from Rachel. A part would go for putting a new show together. The rest saved for Karina and any emergency that might come.

A week had passed when Karin entered the kitchen with a sublime smile while I washed the dishes and left me amazed. Her breast oozed milk as Karina contently suckled.

Now with Karina to care for and winter not too far off, we decided to wait at least another year before trying to get a show on the road. In the meantime, we would start working out novel ideas. The show needed something different, something new to add pizzazz.

Fall arrived in all its splendor. The leaves of the trees covered the mountains and hillsides in brilliant colors. Scarecrows and pumpkins lined the fields. The harvest moon in the evening gave a finishing touch to the magnificent background. God making Himself so present wherever you looked, making it easy to understand why the pilgrims created Thanksgiving.

It also brought my mind back to meditation, and I decided the time had come to make a sincere effort. A better chance I would never have. Meditation remained uneventful and difficult, but I would not desist. In the beginning, Karin remained neutral on spiritual matters. Inquisitive, but not convinced. Many nights she meditated along with me, more as a supportive companion than as a believer. That alone to me was priceless. But soon meditation for her became as routine and normal as eating. While I still struggled, it just effortlessly flowed for her.

A week before Thanksgiving, a package arrived. Rarely did I ever receive something delivered, and this one was for Rachel.

The driver explained, "First we delivered it to the East Side, New York City, in care of Rachel. But she was not there to sign for it. The caretaker of the apartment gave us this address saying, 'She is away and didn't know when she would return.'"

"A long way to go for a small package. You came all this way just to deliver this package?"

"No, we had a large delivery to make not too far from here and brought the package along being that you were so close by."

Karin served lunch for the driver and his helper, and as they left gave them a nice tip for being so thoughtful.

We opened the package because the driver mentioned that it was perishable. There was a note inside with the cookies and sweets, "I hope you enjoy them," signed Mother Smithers. Karin and I both thought it strange since I knew no one that lived in the East Side of New York City and nobody by the name of Smithers. Karin saved the address label. We put the basket aside until Thanksgiving in case Rachel appeared, but she never did.

In early December we went to New York City to shop, visit friends, and stay overnight. Karin had other plans as well which she did not reveal to me. We had a reunion on the Lower West Side with our circus friends and past workers, replete with Christmas presents we brought for them. The next morning, I went to see about buying equipment while Karin went to spend part of the day with Karina by the water. We would meet at four o'clock on Wall Street.

Later in the afternoon when we met, Karin related to me what she did with a gleam in her eye. "I went to the address on the East Side where the package had been first sent to Rachel and I stayed a distance off and waited. An hour later, still in the morning, Rachel walked out the front of the building and took a carriage. When she rode out of view, I went to the two-story house and knocked on the door, and talked with the owner and told him, "I have a package to deliver to Rachel is she home." He replied, "No, she just left a moment ago." I then asked if her husband was in and he replied, "No, he left for work early." I then asked, "I would like to leave a note. Would you mind if I put it under her door?" He replied, "No problem, it is right up the stairway." I thanked him and went to see the name on the door. It was Alfred Smithers. On the way out, I questioned, "Is this the same Alfred that was here several years ago?" He replied, "Yes, they both have been here over a year and a half."

Andrew, can you believe it? She threw all your money away on Alfred. We do not have to worry about getting the divorce anymore, thanks to Mother Smither's cookies. She lived with Alfred before you met Kitty. She cannot do anything against you.

Hugging her I beamed with joy, "Besides being intelligent and courageous, your intuition is incredible." What a wonderful soul that has blessed my life.

In the background of my mind came the remembrance of Kitty's comment about Rachel and the bible always in her hand, "You know what she reads, but do you know what she thinks." The power of a women's subtle intuition, I reflected, is far beyond anything than I ever imagined.

Snow covered the ground January 3rd, the day we believed that Karina came into the world. A calm child with glowing eyes accented by silky blond hair that looked just like Karin's beautiful hair. Karina enjoyed the birthday festivities and all the attention. Acquaintances never knew if Karin was just staying here as she did sometimes in the past or was living with me. A dire sin.

13: NEW BEGINNINGS

The month of January passed quickly. It was Valentine's Day and Rachel arrived with a folder full of papers. We were in the middle of an extended January thaw. She kindly informed us, "We were to meet with her and Father Braun at one o'clock to discuss a divorce." Her arrival did not surprise us, and we agreed to the meeting and invited her to stay for dinner. She declined, "Saying that she had much to do beforehand." Heavier than ever, Rachel lost her youthful appearance. She seemed so unhappy.

Entering the church where Rachel and I had married, Father Braun greeted us cordially. We sat around an old oak table and the Father began the interview looking at Karin and questioning her, "Did this child come from Andrew?" She thought for a moment and replied, "No." Thinking to herself it was Kitty whom the baby came from, not Andrew.

"You liar!" blurted Rachel, as the Father asked us all to remain calm and remember we were in a house of God and to tell the truth.

"Are you sure?" he questioned.

"Yes, I am sure."

Father Braun continued, "Were you living together when the baby arrived?"

"No."

Rachel ranted on, "What's the difference who she was? He lived with another woman and had a baby with her. He's a sinner and adulterer and I want a divorce."

"Andrew had you been, or have you been living here with another woman?"

I thought about his question and following Karin's way of interpreting the questions, I replied, "No." For I reasoned to myself that I traveled with Kitty, but never lived here with her, or anyone else besides Rachel at the time.

"Have you been spending money on other women?" The questions continued and all my answers were no. Rachel was ready to explode.

He finally questioned, "Andrew, where did the baby come from?"

"Father Braun, A lady I met traveling back to states from Europe about two years ago, came here in August, left the baby with me, and just remarked, 'I would make a better father than she could a mother and just like that she left the baby.' Rachel is a witness to this."

But she also said, "She will always remember the enjoyable time you two had together. Didn't she?"

"Yes, she did, I meet many people in my travels and have enjoyable times together. I'm a showman."

"Andrew, do you honestly know for sure where this baby came from?"

"No, I am not." Thinking to myself, it honestly could be someone else's baby, how was I to know for sure? Father Braun's questions left ample room for double-talking on our part. I figured that is okay, I will pay the karma another day if what I am doing is wrong. It is convenient how rationalizing can make it so easy to justify one's actions.

"Rachel do you have any proof Karina came from Andrew."

"No, why do I need proof? It's so obvious?"

"I cannot condemn someone and grant a divorce without concrete proof. Now would you like to add something to this," the Father questioned looking at Karin and me?

Karin responded, "Yes Father, I would. You have known me since my youth and I have always trusted in you, Andrew and Rachel too, until recently when I discovered another side to her." Karin went on explaining about the package we received before Thanksgiving addressed to Rachel, with a note from Mother Smithers. Rachel's hands began trembling.

"Father, Rachel has been living with another man for almost two years. This began shortly after Andrew left for his European tour. His name is Alfred Smithers, and he lives at this address on the East Side, New York. They both live there. Look at this bank account. It had Andrew's life savings in it from all his years of arduous work, over five thousand dollars. This angelic woman here spent it all on Alfred. Well, not all she left Andrew ten dollars. She told him she was paying for her sick sister's medical bills, but a sick sister does not exist."

"Father, she's lying, it's all lies, nothing but lies. I don't know any Alfred Smithers."

Karin then opened documents from a lawyer in New York confirming the two lived in the same apartment.

Fuming with anger and in utter despair, "I'm being framed, it's a conspiracy!" Rachel repeated as she ran out and slammed the old oak door.

The calm atmosphere of the church returned, and Karin asked, "Will you grant Andrew a divorce?" After careful recollection, he nodded with approval.

Inwardly I felt sad for Rachel and with a little guilt, feeling I was partially to blame for the situation. Although pleased that she had inadvertently freed us.

We gave our marriage vows in front of Father Braun four months later. Friends, neighbors, and circus friends gathered at our home for the festivities.

To my surprise, TJ Tall, an expert on the trapeze, came over and gave me his usual backbreaking hug. His name was an antonym for a short man built like a locomotive. For years I had not seen him, and we never worked together. But at that moment I realized that is the something different we need for the show, the pizzazz that I had been looking for. TJ related that he, like the rest of them, had been out of work and would do anything. We got together with B Bob the clown, an artist with horse riding tricks, and our other circus friends. Before the day ended, we had all the help we needed to get the show on the road.

Karin and I had already been buying equipment and supplies, planning to get a show going. During the past winter months, we built all the props we would need to do our magic show.

And then a wonderful surprise to finish a perfect day. Our circus cook and mother to all of us, Miss Maria arrived. A loveable character and unsung star of the circus. We bathed her in hugs and kisses. What a relief to know she would be with us again.

Her silent applause came from all those that came to the circus and delighted in her popcorn. Mouthwatering, salted and buttered with a hint of delicate savory spice. For extra melted dripping butter, one only had to ask. Her recipe so different, so good, no one resisted… again and again. Every night we all hoped plenty would be leftover; that she forced us to eat, not wanting any waste. There were days we took in more money on the popcorn than the ticket sales.

Watching over all of us and whenever the insidious workings of gossip or misunderstanding paid a visit to her door, she snatched them up, bound and buried them before they spread their disease. A few firm but kind words of counsel to the maker, and peace returned. We all loved her dearly.

14: THE SHOW BEGINS

Now that TJ Tall would join the show, we would need a new larger tent with reinforced main poles to support the trapeze and perches. It would take several months to make, so we planned a September start in New York. Then work our way southwards for the winter months. Concerned about the worker's unpaid bills, I advanced them three months of salary.

TJ Tall stayed and made a trapeze with a safety net in the yard where he and Karin could begin training. Karin had trained in the past on the trapeze, although never did a live performance. She had just turned thirty years old, but she flew through the air with the agility of an eighteen-year-old. TJ Tall had the strength to compensate for any misjudgments in timing.

B Bob the clown arrived a week later with his three horses and Amazon Eric the strong man. We built a circular arena for B Bob to train. The last touches on my magic equipment were taking shape. It looked like we would have the best circus ever. Everyone had grand expectations. We harbored no plans to compete with the big-time circuses; we had a niche of our own.

A seamstress designed and sewed colorful outfits. We built new portable benches and bought extra wagon wheels.

We faced our share of setbacks, but we managed to have an opening night on September 12th in New York. The constant standing applause and whistling during and at the final curtain confirmed it all for the success of the show. It gave us all a feeling of relief and heartwarming accomplishment. After ten days we moved on to Pennsylvania and took a rest in Lancaster, then onto Virginia and the Carolinas. Traveling as far as Texas, we then began a return route to New York. We only stopped for one day to celebrate Karina's birthday. We arrived exhausted from the constant work and travel in late June and rested for two months, passing up the lucrative summer months. We planned to begin again in the fall until the first snow, then rest during the winter instead of going south. Then after the spring thaw, we would begin in the Northeast going through the northern states and then in September head south. The next three years passed quickly.

The fourth year, because of a lingering winter, we were still at home in May. The roads were muddy and almost impassable for wagons. The warm days were delightful, and Karina loved to play bouncing on the safety net, under the trapeze in the yard. One day sitting and enjoying a picnic lunch that the Johnsons brought, Karin in despair shouted out, "No, No!" Karina now six and a half years old, had climbed up onto the high trapeze perch. Without a second thought, she jumped down to the safety net bouncing and laughing. Karin gave her a good scolding. We all felt shook-up afterward and wondered how to keep Karina away from the trapeze. Except for taking it down, no one gave a workable suggestion.

Days passed, and the scene kept repeating. Karina loved the trapeze and seemed to know nothing of fear. One day TJ Tall came to visit and after hearing about Karina's exploits remarked, "Don't worry, it is the perfect age to learn the trapeze."

Thinking, oh yeah, it is easy to say when the child is someone else's. But Karin took it to heart. The next day she let Karina go up on the perch with her. She then swung through the air with Karina hanging on. I never saw a happier child.

Days passed, and they continued playing until Karin started thinking seriously about letting Karina do something simple with her during a show. Firmly, I remained against the idea. However, they paid no attention to me. Training every day, they soon had perfect timing and synchronization with each other in the air. Already planning their first act, Karin would swing close to the perch and with a short falling forward motion, Karina would grab her mother's feet. They were a beautiful site to see in the air together.

To admit I was wrong without saying anything, I asked the seamstress to secretly make a costume for Karina. A better gift I could not have given her as they both hugged me, then rushed to Karina's room. Afterward they went right up on the trapeze and together did their act with her new outfit, and I applauded. They were a natural duo together. They kept practicing nonstop doing their acrobatics.

The roads finally dried and were passable. B Bob the clown showed up and later TJ Tall arrived. We would hit the road the following week. In the days that followed, TJ started becoming difficult and creating arguments with the tent handlers and B Bob over nothing. It was so unlike him. The last thing we needed was disharmony between us, as we lived together day and night when traveling. Even Miss Maria could not resolve the problem. Finally, I sat to talk with him.

"TJ what's wrong?" In a caring manner, I questioned him.

He replied impatiently, "Listen here, I have been watching your daughter and wife on the trapeze, and if you think I will work with a little girl up there you are mistaken."

"You don't have to, let her do a little something with Karin. I thought you liked her playing on the trapeze."

"Playing is one thing, but I will not share the show with a little girl and that's it. You decide Andrew it is her or me." Hours passed as I tried to reason with him, but to no avail and he finally demanded, "Either she goes, or I go."

"TJ, I would like her to stay. Everyone thinks she is a delightful addition to your act. It's not to take anything away from you."

"I'm out of here. I don't need you. A lot of new circuses have started." He packed up his things and left. I thought Karin and everyone else would be angry with me, but they were not.

The next day I decided it was time to change the name of the circus. It was not just "The Great Oswell" anymore. I did not want to make too much of a change as we were well known by that name. Amazon Eric began repainting all the signs and wagons with "The Great Oswells," and with two ladies swinging on a trapeze.

Later in the afternoon Karin and Karina went out to the big barn where we stored the circus equipment. Amazon Eric had just finished painting when Karina and Karin arrived and saw the new signs. Overjoyed, they hugged me tight with their unspoken approval. As usual, they teased Erick, this time about how delicate his workmanship was for such a strong man. Eric enjoyed their teasing.

15: LADIES AND GENTLEMEN

We started in New York for our opening night. B Bob's clowning antics left everyone laughing uproariously in the moments between acts. Besides the horses and dogs, we had no cages and no animals; except for one, a cage for Amazon Erick the Wildman. He was the circus strongman. Before the start of the show, we would leave him chained in a cage near the stage, ranting and grunting, shaking the cage wildly. While B Bob was in the middle of his clowning antics Amazon Erick would break loose, jump up on the stage, and grab B Bob. Frightened faces shrieked as he threw B Bob high in the air; luckily landing in the trapeze safety net. Karin in her delicate outfit, typical of a circus performer, would unafraid walk up to Amazon Erick while he grunted and flexed his giant muscles, threatening the nervous audience. Looking eye to eye with him, Karin would lightly slap him on the face. Amazon Eric would fall to his knees crying and saying, "You hit me!" to an uproar of laughter. Standing up, he would begin his incredible powerlifting show.

The best response came from the audience when Karin would stand against a wooden backdrop blindfolded with her arms straight out along the backdrop, her ankles and wrists locked in place. Throwing knives only inches from her body, sometimes two at a time, shocking the audience, and sometimes throwing one knife way off target to make it more realistic, although all only an illusion. In the rest of my magic show, I used unseen mirrors, making things disappear and of sleight-of-hand tricks that kept the audience spellbound. The horses and clowns added a nice entertaining touch to the show.

Ladies and Gentlemen: Karin and Karina

Tonight, however, all eyes were on a tiny six-year-old climbing up to the trapeze perch. Absolute silence reigned as she stood up, waiting to grasp Karin's feet as she swiftly flew by. Karina misjudged and went straight down to the safety net. The audience shrieked. Karina unceremoniously slid off the net and climbed right back up to the perch. Karin swung by again, and they began their routine in perfect unison. The applause at the end became an uproar. The circus had a new star. All our eyes were wet with tears of joy. What a celebration that followed. We traveled on and their act became increasingly sophisticated.

16: THE RAILROAD DOCTOR

We were in Indiana heading to Saint Louis, Missouri when Karin started having severe pains in her abdomen. We knew of no nearby city. Karina and I were anxious as I had never seen Karin sick, in all the time I had known her. Or at least she never once mentioned being ill. The next morning gave her no relief. I asked B Bob to take a horse and ride ahead and see if he could find a doctor somewhere. We continued traveling on behind him. Two days later B Bob returned and said that there is a big crew working on the railroad. There are a lot of Chinese workers, and they have a doctor with them.

We arrived at the railroad site a day later and asked the foreman about the doctor and he just chuckled. "What was so funny," I asked.

"He ain't no normal doctor, he's a witch doctor. Only the Chinese trust him and his potions."

"Is there another doctor around these parts?"

"Yeah, he lives about fifty miles from here."

"It will take too long. Can we meet with the Chinese doctor?"

"Sure, come with me."

"He led us to the doctor's tent."

The doctor was all smiles, nodding his head often but saying nothing. How we would ever explain anything to him, I wondered. The doctor motioned for us to sit down. Then in a heavily accented English, he spoke to Karin, "Hold out your hand." That gave a relief at least we could talk with him.

Asking the Doctor his name, he replied, "John."

Surprised, I asked, "John?"

"Jianyu, but the boss man calls me Dr. John."

He took her hand commenting, "I want to feel your pulse." He then put one of his fingers gently on her wrist and closed his eyes. After several minutes he said, "Yes." He then stared unblinking in Karin's eyes for quite a while. "Please lie down over here," he asked Karin.

After she lied down, he mentioned, "I need to apply oils to her kidneys and bladder and need her abdomen exposed. Would you mind opening her dress, you can cover her with this cloth?" He applied fragrant oils, lots of them, some very astringent. In between his massaging, he prepared teas that he gave her to drink and plenty of them. Frequently he stopped and sat with his eyes closed as if meditating. Karin fell asleep in the middle of all this. I did not know if it was the effect of one of the potent teas or the pain finally subsided by itself.

The afternoon had passed when Dr. Jianyu finally spoke, "She will be well when she wakes. She has a small, but a very sharp stone that had come out of her kidney. After she wakes, it should wash out when she relieves herself of all the liquids she has been drinking."

"A stone I questioned; how could she have eaten a stone?" He then explained to me how stones can form in the kidneys. It was all new to me.

Karin woke a short while later and the first thing she said, I need to go to.... Before she finished the doctor led her out to a nearby tree out of the view of the rest of the camp. There were no private toilets for a woman. She gave a muffled scream, I jumped up to help, but the doctor held my hand and commented that it is an excellent sign. Karin returned very pale after what seemed a long time and questioned, "Lots of blood came out in the urine. Am I dying?"

The doctor replied, "How are you feeling?"

"Being so worried about the blood I didn't realize the pain almost stopped. Will I be okay?"

"Yes, I believe you already are. The blood was from a small trapped, very jagged and sharp stone, it should have passed." He then explained to Karin what he already explained to me about kidney stones.

Karin then questioned, "Will it happen again?"

"I cannot be sure, but I don't think so. This one may have been there for a long while, perhaps from a time in your life when you suffered difficulties. One can never be sure, but your kidney appears clean. Take these herbs with you, should this ever happen again."

"Why do you feel it is now clean?"

"Just intuition."

After thanking the doctor, "I asked him how much it would be?"

"I don't charge for helping people."

"Why not?"

"I'm already paid by the boss man and it is a blessing I can cure someone. I also don't like to see God suffer."

"Sorry doctor, but I don't get it. How is it God is suffering; Karin felt the pain?"

"Do you not realize that God suffers along with us through all our trials and pains?

"He does? Are you sure?"

"Yes, how could he not? He is as much a part of us as we are. You cannot separate man from God. Not physically, spiritually, or mentally. Nor can you separate God from any aspect of Nature."

"If that is true then why does He just not prevent all the pain and suffering of mankind? What's the point?"

"If He prevented all the pain and suffering of mankind caused by our wrong and evil actions, our learning process would end. The binding and blinding forces of Maya, and the forces of karma, would serve no purpose, evolution would stop, and the cosmos would have no further reason to exist. What motive would we have to be good? Why not just kill and steal?

"The problem for us is that we don't remember all the good and bad karma that we have accumulated over past lives. Not knowing the distant past, it is hard to understand the just rewards we are receiving today for what we have done, good or bad.

"That is not to say He does not help. Our answered prayers often go unnoticed, because we have preconceived expectations of how He should help, and what the results should be. But He knows what we need to learn and what is best for us, and as a result His silent help often remains unnoticed."

In the Hindu fashion of greeting or thanking someone, I bowed to him with hands clasped. He looked at me with astonishment. "Doctor thanks, I have been wrestling with this dilemma for a long time." He gave a knowing smile.

In the back of my mind was the frustration I had when I escaped onto Kitty's ship and the great deception that I had with God for not preventing all I went through. It was something I tried to accept out of blind faith, but the doubt remained ever undiminished.

The doctor suggested that Karin not travel in the bumpy carriage for several days. He offered his tent for us and mentioned that he would sleep elsewhere. We accepted the invitation and left him a well-deserved monetary gift.

"Doctor, what did you mean about the blinding and binding forces of Maya?"

"Maya makes everything that exists seem so real."

"I thought everything was real."

"No. In reality, everything is just God's dream. Maya makes the dream appear real."

"It's hard to imagine it is all a dream when someone is sick like Karin. The pain does not go away like a dream. How is that possible?"

"Would you like to talk about it later?"

"Yes, as Karin nodded her head in agreement."

"Then I will return this evening after you all have rested awhile."

17: NARADA

Later in the evening Dr. Jianyu returned and questioned Karin, "How are you feeling?"

"Like a new person doctor."

"Good, I'm pleased."

"The food is still warm I brought. When I asked the boss man if I could bring you food, he said, 'No problem, they seem like a nice family.'"

Famished from not stopping to cook all day, the beans and rice with the oriental flavorings tasted like ambrosia. This was the first meal Karin had eaten in days.

"Can I tell you a short story I once heard when I was living in the Himalayan Mountains about Narada?" Dr. Jianyu asked.

Karina loved to listen to the stories about saints and yogis that I told her at night before going to bed, enthusiastically she replied, "Please go ahead."

Well, long, long ago in ancient India Lord Krishna had incarnated. A disciple of his, Narada, came to visit him. Narada was a very advanced soul. He had transcended all of God's tests.

Sometimes he would stay in the glorious astral world and sometimes he would go to God's home in the transcendental world of endless bliss beyond our cosmos. Or he would stay in the higher, subtle realms of the Angels. Sometimes he would visit our Earth.

A sylvan forest found them walking along in silent understanding, so happy to be together. Narada finally spoke, "Master, could you please teach me about Maya?"

"Narada, you already know everything about Maya," he replied."

"No, I don't."

"Yes, you do."

"I'm not sure I understand."

"Narada forget this idea of yours."

"But I want to know, it has been so long since I felt it."

"Narada, trust me and forget this notion of yours."

The subject forgotten, they walked for hours enjoying the sylvan beauty. Krishna finally sat near a ledge overlooking a distant valley and asked Narada, "Would you mind getting me a cup of water?"

"Not at all, he responded." A disciple considers it an honor to do anything for a true Master.

Narada set off on the trail and walked and walked for a long time. The forest trail led to a valley of rolling hills. Walking on, he came to a clearing. A woman stood there with her back turned to him, taking water from a well with a large bucket on a rope.

"Hello, may I have a cup of water please," he asked.

As she turned to see who spoke, her beautiful long black hair just swayed in the gentle breeze. She was the most beautiful woman he had ever seen, her eyes shown of divinity. She answered in the sweetest voice, "Yes, but I don't have a cup here. You will have to come to my house. Would you mind?"

"No, I won't mind," replied Narada.

They walked to her home and as they walked and talked Narada fell deeper and deeper in love with her.

Her father hearing someone approaching the house appeared on the veranda. Before he spoke, Narada with a heart full of passion announced, "I want to marry your daughter."

With calm eyes, the father looked down at Narada and could see he was a spiritualized soul with an aura of peace. He finally answered, "You know, I have been looking for a husband for my daughter Sarah. Under one condition I would consent."

Before he could continue, Narada in an excited, cheerful voice remarked, "Anything, what would you like? The sun, the moon, a gold mine, just tell me what you wish, and it is yours."

The father interrupted, saying, "None of that, I am getting old, and I am the head of the village. The elders depend on me to solve the problems and difficulties that arise here. Sometimes they are difficult to resolve. You must promise you will help me, and later take over my responsibilities when I die."

"It would be an honor, I would be glad to," Narada responded.

His daughter enchanted with Narada became overjoyed with the day's surprising events. Immediately they began making their marriage plans.

A month later pronounced man and wife. The entire village celebrated the festive event. One year later their first child arrived, a boy with a happy radiance. Another year passed and blessed them with a daughter. Just like their mother and father, they were both of a highly spiritualized nature. Their life together was in perfect spiritual harmony. Narada proved to be an excellent negotiator resolving the conflicts and problems that arose in the community.

He implemented the construction of a large dam to hold back the rains from the monsoons, and to have continuous water for irrigation. After the monsoons, several months of the year passed in a drought where they lived. The dam would resolve the problem.

The inauguration celebrations of the finished dam lasted for days. His boy was now five years old, and the girl was four years old.

A month later the monsoons arrived, bringing heavy rains. The reservoir was already reaching close to its full capacity. Narada and his family were sitting around the fireplace enjoying delicacies Sarah had prepared. This evening the rains were extremely heavy, nothing like they had ever seen before. Narada expressed concern because the dam had never been at full capacity before, and the small tributaries were turning into swollen rivers. Leaving to see how the dam was holding up, he opened the door to leave, but the water was already on top of the veranda.

He called for Sarah and his children to leave with him and go to higher ground. Immediately they left the house holding hands. They had taken a few steps when hearing a thunderous roar, they realized the dam broke and in an instant, an enormous wall of water crashed upon them, sweeping them away together in the violent swirling waters. The boy's hand lost his grip, and he went under. Narada went after him, searching under the muddy black water. He swam and swam until his lungs felt they would burst. He came back up for air, then swam and searched until his arms gave out. The force of the water threw him against a ledge. He grappled to get hold. He tried and tried to hold on to the slippery rock, his fingers bleeding and torn to the bone. Finally, he got a grip and pulled himself up. He looked and looked but to no avail. In vain he cried out for Sarah and his children, with no reply. The village destroyed, everything in shambles, no one survived. His head on his knees, he just cried and cried. It is all my fault. How was it possible my trying to help and do only the best possible good I created so much pain and destruction, destroying everything I loved?

He could not go on living and was about to take his life when he heard a voice… "Narada, where is my cup of water?"

No one spoke as Dr. Jianyu sat quietly for a few moments. He then continued, "Most of my studies were in China, but I also studied Ayurvedic medicine in India. There I had a professor who acknowledged, 'Only yoga can free you from Maya's seemingly insurmountable delusive power.'"

"He called the cosmos we live in the city of Emperidone and elucidated that life's only goal is to escape Emperidone. However, Maya casts a Bittersweet Veil of Illusion in the cosmos that beguiles and mystifies us through desires and the dualities of pain and pleasure, hot and cold, health and sickness. Hiding the Infinite Essence of Peace, Joy, and Love."

He also avowed, "For unseen and unfelt surrounding Emperidone is the subtle heaven of God's boundless love and bliss. So wondrous and satisfying that once tasted all other desires melt away. Meditation is the mystical force that can lead one to the luminous doorway that un-blinds and un-binds those imprisoned in Emperidone. It is the only way to escape to that heavenly realm, our true nature - guided by the blessings of God and Guru."

Sitting quietly as Karin and Karina lied down to sleep, in the light of the flickering oil lantern, I stared at a small table next to Dr. Jianyu's improvised bed. A quill pen next to an inkwell shared the space with several sheets of paper held in place by a small statue of Buddha. Wondering if more knowledge and healing left this table than many of the great laboratories?

18: JUSTIN

The following year passed so fast. Karina, now almost eight years old, matured quickly during this time both as a performer and an enchanting young girl. In three weeks, we would begin our tour from New York heading west.

We could not head south as we always did in the past. Sadly, the civil war had begun on April 12, 1861, when Confederate forces attacked a U.S. military installation at Fort Sumter in South Carolina.

Karina could not understand the concept of war and became very distraught that we could not travel south. She loved it down there. Karin born in Louisiana had that warm southern charm. In the North, her southern hospitality won over the coldest heart. Down south the people treated us more like close friends than circus workers. Whenever we set up in cities that had nearby plantations, we made a special showing for the slaves. Those with limited understanding questioned our motives. But over the years we got to know many of the plantation owners and the special showings became a welcomed ritual. They treated Karina and Karin like angels from heaven. It was not too hard to understand Karina's great deception with the war. She too wanted the slaves free, but not by war and killing.

We were sitting in the backyard garden when hearing a carriage coming up the drive, Karina ran to the front of the house. Karin and I remained behind to let Karina receive the visitor, which she loved to do. When my brother Justin came around the corner of the house hand in hand with Karina, I could not believe my eyes. He wore a smile and a cowboy hat. Jumping up to greet him, we just hugged each other and said nothing. How I had missed him."

"Who is this angelic little girl here?"

"That's our daughter Karina."

"You're married?"

"Yes, this is Karin."

"Wow, it's a pleasure to meet you, I'm Justin Andrew's younger brother."

"Andrew in the past told me a lot about you, always pleasant things."

"Well, you must be hungry. If you need anything, I will be in the kitchen making lunch, while you both can get caught up on the past."

"Justin I can't believe you're here. It's over 12 years since I last saw you."

"Andrew, what a beautiful wife and daughter you have, I am so happy for you. Whatever happened to Rachel?"

"She ran off with another man when I was in Europe almost eight years ago. Karin and I then got married." Before I could continue Karin called out from the kitchen window, "Put Justin's bags in the guest room and let him wash up."

"And Leticia, did you ever marry her? She was such a sweet girl."

"Yes, we got married and we are still together. No children, but we've done all right for ourselves."

While we were eating, I asked Justin, "Where did you finally end up living? Mom and dad were crying the last time I saw you as you headed out the door going west in search of gold."

"California, Andrew, California, people have come from around the world to make it big time. You would love it. Everything is beautiful. The scenery, the people, the vineyards, and orchards, it is incredible. Well, it is different today than when I went there during the gold rush. Then it was hostile, with violence and killing. Tons of gold just waited in those hills and streams, and people got rich overnight.

"But that is all in the past, and the wealth that stayed behind is building a new world there. Besides those of us from the States, people came from everywhere dreaming of instant wealth, China, Latin America, Japan, Europe. Being one of the lucky ones, I found gold in a secluded little mountain stream and lots of it. My hardest job was hiding it. I took no chances and put it in a bunch of different banks. Afterward, I counted my blessings and went to San Francisco.

"Although I wanted you to come out and join me, there was no way to let you know. Getting mail from California to the East Coast was too difficult. That is when I started thinking about communications. The future is in communications, I said to myself, then started studying and investing in the telegraph. The business I started became an enormous success. The company is putting up lines everywhere in the West.

"It's not just the telegraph. In 1849 when I arrived in California, it took four tough months with suffering to get there, and many of those traveling with me died. Coming here, I traveled part of the way comfortably on trains and with decent food. And it will not be long before they finish the transcontinental railroad. You can also get on a steamer from San Francisco going to Panama, then an easy connection heading up to the east coast ports, fast and comfortable. Do you see the future of technology?"

"I've been on steamers and a train, but never used the telegraph, but I passed many situations where it would have been a blessing to send an instant message to someone far away. I'm sure Karin would agree it would have saved endless difficulties for us."

"With the transatlantic cable, you can send a message to England, France, Germany, and lots of other places and it will get delivered the same day. The news goes back and forth instantly between Europe and the United States. Andrew, I will tell you, I envision the day when there will be a telegraph in every city and even homes. You do not even have to be there to receive a message. Electromagnetic printers print out the message on thin paper spools that you can save and read anytime.

"Andrew, it's a booming business. It would be nice to have a partner like you I could trust. You can make it big time. It will be an enjoyable life for Karin and Karina. No hurry, think about it, and when you decide, let me know."

"Thanks, Justin, that's tempting. But I know little about running a business, besides the circus."

"If you can run a circus with all the hardships and difficulties, you can help manage my business, I mean our business. You can have them both. Bring the circus to California and let Karin run it. Talk it over and when you decide, send me a telegram on the new overland telegram service that goes from coast to coast. For now, I will travel, seeing what arrangements I can make with the big boys in the business out here in the East. I just hope this stupid war does not mess things up too much and is over quick. Imagine sending your son down south to kill somebody. It is crazy, simply crazy. Just let the poor slaves go already. And all the money being wasted?"

When we walked out of the kitchen into the living room Justin stopped and stared at the picture over the fireplace mantle.

Before he ridiculed it, I mentioned, "Oh, it's just an actor."

"That's no actor. You don't know what you are messing with. That's Shiva."

Karin and I looked at each other, astonished. I felt a little stupid trying to conceal something I should have been proud of telling Justin and replied, "I was tired of visitors asking who the snake charmer was and asked him how he knew."

"Andrew never be embarrassed having a picture of God on your fireplace or anywhere."

"This is not California Justin, it is New England, puritans, and witches"

"Andrew, New England is the heart of spiritual freedom in the Occident."

"Even so, they're not ready to accept yoga and meditation yet. It only conjures up images of inconceivable gods and fakirs doing strange feats.

"But tell me how you knew?"

"California, Andrew, California, my neighbors in San Francisco came from India. They explain a lot of things to me about meditation and yoga."

"And you believed them?"

"At first no, I thought everything about their way of thinking too abstract."

"See what I mean."

"Yeah, maybe you're right. Anyway, they had answers to the questions about religion that nobody else ever answered for me. Answers that were, well, difficult to deny. Everything they told me about religion always made sense.

"But, Andrew, why did you put up this picture?"

I then related my Himalayan adventure.

"That is incredible, Andrew. Karma, it is totally karma that the two of us ended up attracted to yoga. Unbelievable, I just cannot believe it. It is the law of attraction we both ended up in the same family. Those yogis really know what they are talking about."

It was an enticing idea, going to California and leaving the tents, wagons, and hardships behind. It would be nice to work with a spiritually inclined brother and to live around people that think the same about religion. In San Francisco, working with executives and guaranteed a big income it appeared the ideal life for us all.

Karin was a little standoffish about the subject. After so many years of loneliness before Karina came into our lives, she did not want to risk anything. But I also knew she would support any decision I made, even though I would decide nothing without her heartfelt consent. As we all sat that night meditating I prayed deeply for guidance; that whatever decision we made would be the best for all of us, including Justin and everyone involved with the circus. But no answer came.

The next morning, I told Justin, "The circus would open in a few weeks in New York. He was welcome to stay at our house when he returned from Boston." He thanked us and gave the addresses where we could send telegrams. He also mentioned, "I will pay all the expenses of moving out West."

Later at the train station, before he left for Boston, I assured him, "We will make our decision soon after we get the circus on the road again and see all the possibilities. It's the workers we have to think of too." He understood and did not push the issue.

Three weeks later we received a package from Justin. Overwhelmed with curiosity, Karina pulled apart the package. She found a wrapped-up book and a small drum just like the one in the picture of Shiva. It had a tag hanging from it with a word stamped on it: DAMARU with a written note.

She unraveled the two leather striking cords attached at the middle of the two-headed hourglass-shaped drum. It fit comfortably in her hand. When she twisted her wrist back and forth the polished stone beads at the end of the leather cords striking the drumheads made no sound. She then tried to play tapping with her fingers and still nothing.

Reading the note, "Gently heat the drum skin if it becomes too soft." We stoked up the wood stove and heated the leather drum heads. We then put them back on making them nice and taught with the adjusting cords. The sound returned. Karina started beating discordant sounds. She then wisely went out by the stream to practice with it.

While we fixed the damaru, Karin unwrapped the book. It was a copy of Bhagavad-Gita. It soon became her evening companion, I preferred reading it in the daylight. Karin commented, "We need to send a telegram to Justin next time we are in a big city. What wonderful gifts. Where in the world, did he find them?"

One evening after days of practicing a long way from the house, Karina sat in her room and played the damaru. Karin and I looked at each other, amazed. Enchanting rhythms were coming from Karina's room. Karin sat with her, and they began singing Karin's favorite chant. It did not take long before delightful music was coming from the room with Karin singing while Karina played. Not wanting to frighten the scarecrows with my singing, I did not accompany them. Karina must have played music in a past life, to be so naturally proficient with no one to teach her in such a brief time.

The time to leave had come, and we were on the road with the circus heading to New York but remained undecided about California. The answers I expected from meditation never came. After the show on the second night, one of the tent handlers handed me a folded note from a woman that had paid to see the show but stayed outside looking through the canvass. Finding a quiet spot, I opened the letter.

Dear Andrew,

For the first time, I watched the show tonight. It is the most beautiful sight I have seen in my life, Karina flying through the air with Karin, her outfit sparkling drawing standing ovations. Their loving glances, my heart is in turmoil.

Inside, I am an empty broken person. Possessing everything one can dream of but have become lonely nothingness inside. To have you near me again and the love of Karina, I would sell my soul.

That nothing will interfere with Karina's happiness, I will let none of you see me. I woke up, but it is too late. Can you believe it, I am crying? Remembering this night is the only thing that will keep me alive.

Always yours,
Kitty

Rushing to the outside lot, I could not spot her in the people mulling around the horses and carriages. Searching everywhere, but I could not find Kitty. Turmoil took hold of my mind. If I could have only spoken with her. But then again, her appearance could have changed Karina's life, and life for all of us. Over and over again, I reflected on everything. I felt the same way I did when I hung on the cliff in the Himalayas. So much time and so little realized. It took weeks before I could concentrate again. Resolving from this day forth, I would make a supreme effort on the spiritual path. How Kitty's suffering made me realize how blessed Karin, Karina, and I already were. The risk of our lives changing in California was too great. What could be more valuable than the love and happiness we already had? The answer about California came dramatically. There would be no

California for now. I also noted the Divine responds, but sometimes in a way far different from the expected, and on His own time.

The next day I sent a telegram to Justin thanking him, but that I would not be coming right now. Karin felt relieved about not going to California.

19: NIGHTMARE

Every day thereafter I meditated resolutely, Karina and Karin accompanied me. We had a crinkled, slightly torn picture of Shiva that I had bought in India, different from the one on our fireplace mantle. Wherever we stayed, we hung the framed picture in our tent. Karina had an instant attraction for Shiva from the first time she saw his picture at home. Those who saw it as we traveled figured it was a circus actor, so it did not raise any unusual comments. We made a fervent effort on the spiritual path, being so grateful for all the blessings bestowed on us. Karina daily offered flowers to Shiva and put them by his picture, a heartwarming scene to watch. It brought us so close together.

I thought the day Kitty arrived at my doorstep with Karina in the basket was the end of my life. But it turns out that it was a fresh beginning for me. Karina and Karin opened a channel for love to flow in my life that I never knew before. Their joyous countenance made the transformation in my life effortless on my part. I just absorbed their out-flowing love. I felt like a wilted plant put in a vase of reviving and invigorating water. Without them, I would never have understood spiritual devotion.

Many nights Karina played the damaru while Karen sang along. The rhythm and intonation would sometimes get softer and softer as their devotion deepened, then slowly more intense. In the background of my mind, the music played on long after they stopped. It brought back fond memories of the Temple in the Himalayans. Having the two of them to share a life with, I remained ever thankful for my great fortune.

Two years had now passed since Kitty's visit to the circus. We harbored no regrets about not going to California. Karina trained and trained and became a master of airborne somersaults and attracted throngs wherever we traveled. We found a tutor that lived along with us for Karina, now ten years old.

We decided to return to New England to be closer to home before the weather became too cold. We arrived in Vermont in early October. The high mountains and scenery were magnificent. It was the last night of the show before we would head home. We wanted to have everything put away before the snow started.

The seats sold out. B Bob the clown stood behind a curtain and made drum rolls before the two acrobats began their routine. It gave a nice added touch to the show. Karina was up top chalking her hands when we heard thunder in the distance. A short downpour wetted the canvas and poles, a few brisk gusts of wind, and then all remained calm. Karin was swinging gently back and forth as Karina concentrated on the perch.

Suddenly a crash of thunder overhead and a blinding flash. Lightning exploded on the support pole, violently throwing Karina backward from the high perch away from the safety net. She hit the ground with a heart-sickening thud. All were aghast at the horrific sight. In a flash, I kneeled over her. Broken and burnt, her feet were just bare bones. A doctor in the crowd came running over; he put his head to her chest. His eyes left no hope as he stood up and silently walked away.

Kneeling, Karin picked up Karina's lifeless form in her arms. There was no consolation one could offer. We sat in the frigid night air in disbelief. Why, oh why? She hurt no one or anything and loved by all. We felt so close to God, only to end up abandoned by Him.

It was not until early morning when Karin passed out that we could pick up Karina and put her in some blankets. B Bob and the others first bandaged up her feet and cleaned her up the best they could. They knew Karin would not part with her on the long trip home.

The doctor returned at dawn. He recommended burying the body here in Vermont before leaving. Karin awoke hearing the conversation and picked Karina up. They tried talking to Karin, but she was in a comatose state, unresponsive. She would not let go of Karina. In a state of shock, I was not much better.

We headed back home and fortunately with the frigid weather Karina's corpse did not noticeably deteriorate on the way. B Bob arranged a funeral for Karina and Father Braun covered her with earth.

20: AFTERMATH

Tortured by an unforgiving nightmare, the invisible tentacles of delusion reached into our minds and unleashed their lethal venom. Karin just sat without eating or talking. Neither of us ate since that night. We both just wanted to be alone, to not exist.

Karin burned within, the fire consuming her heart. Losing what she most loved in the world and abandoned by God, lifeless, she sat day after day, mourning the past, lamenting the future.

The dear Johnsons kept up the house and kept the wood stove stoked. Ingrid made food for us, which just sat untouched day after day. They looked after us as best they could, while slowly day by day we wasted away getting weaker and weaker.

Finally, one day fearing for Karin's life, I kissed her on the forehead and said, come let us walk by the brook; it was Karina's favorite spot. She consented to my surprise, but when she tried to get up, she could not she was so weak. "You need to eat, or you won't get out to where Karina played." I brought her the soup Ingrid had left us. We both slowly sipped the soup. Even swallowing was difficult.

It revitalized us enough to walk outside, a great accomplishment. The soup made us even hungrier, and I made oatmeal porridge with maple syrup. A little shine appeared on Karin's dull eyes.

After eating she finally spoke, "Why Andrew, why?" She was a harmless person. She did no wrong. It is just not fair. We sat and prayed to God together every day. Meditated and prayed with such devotion, for what, that He can turn around and kill her? I regret praying to Shiva, the God of destruction. What a mistake. Our prayers killed her. What have we done? If it would bring her back, I would kill myself right now. And if it were not for you, I would have done it already. Andrew hold me, I embraced her. "Say something," she inconsolably asked. But I could not think of one thing to say of encouragement and answered, "I love you both."

From that day on, we continued eating and regaining our vigor. After two weeks, we looked a little less like walking skeletons, but the inner torment remained ever undiminished.

Months passed, and we regained our weight, but we still looked old and haggard. Karin harbored an intense resentment for the lord Shiva, and me for bringing Him into our lives. I knew no way to defend the Lord. Although she tried to bury it deep inside, it was devouring her. Our life together was dull and monotonous. Her unspoken resentment was eating up the love and affection she once showered on me.

The circus ended. Each one received a year of pay in compensation, and I told them they could have all the tents and equipment. I just wanted to have everything removed and out of sight. There would be no more circus or magic. It brutally ended all that brought happiness into our life.

21: AWAKENING

Although we slept in the same bed, it was as if strangers. Karin treated me cordially but without affection. Depressed, she seemed to live in a distant world. We both kept ourselves busy doing chores here and there around the homestead, anything to divert our thoughts from the tragedy that remained glued in our minds. We went to bed early on this cold February evening. After filling the woodstove, I gave an unresponsive kiss on Karin's forehead before covering myself.

In the middle of the night, I awoke, after having a dream of Karina. It was so real, only to find Karin sitting up in bed next to me. She told me she just had a dream of Karina that was so vivid. Suddenly, a bright figure appeared in front of the bed. An angel glowed in the moonlit room. The last vision I had of her was in Barbados. We both were seeing the angel as if she materialized in front of us. Karina appeared at her side with the sweetest smile. Karin started to jump forward to hug Karina, but the angel held up her hand and said, "Wait," in her angelic voice.

Mommy, Daddy, "I miss you so much." Karina's eyes glistened as she spoke. "Please do not cry for me, I am so happy in a wonderful world. It is a beautiful place where everything and everyone is in perfect harmony." Karina's voice was as though ethereal. Everything conveyed and understood intuitively. Just like with Ran Baja with my vision in the Himalayas.

"When I left the earth, it happened so fast I felt no pain, nothing. In the blissful ecstasy emanating from Shiva, I awoke.

"It is a special place in the astral world. He told me that with my karma I was not supposed to die on that day. But yes, an accident was to happen, and I was to remain painfully paralyzed for many years. However, because of all our devotion and spiritual efforts meditating, I was spared all that pain and suffering.

"In this world, I feel all the pains and happiness of those that think of me. I constantly feel your sadness, and it makes me so unhappy. I have so much love for you both and pray for you every day, I wish you could feel it. The sadness I have would instantly leave if you would be happy.

"Please do not resent Lord Shiva, He watches over you and shows me the both of you often. Mom, He understands your feeling of resentment and knows it is only because you do not understand, and He also knows it is not easy for you. Shiva has told me we will all be together again. Meditate that I can feel the joy you brought into my life."

The angel then touched Karin and me, and we both saw the world where Karina had gone too. Precious time to hug Karina, an everlasting memory. Just a glimpse of a wondrous world beyond, but it gave an untold understanding. Afterward, Karin and I hugged each other and did not let go, our pillows soaked with tears.

Nothing would ever diminish the love and the emptiness we

felt by our separation from Karina. But now we knew a joy that made the trials bearable.

When we awoke in the morning, we took the picture of Shiva out of the closet, dusted it, and placed it on a desk in Karina's room. This would be our temple. Fresh pine in a vase adorned the picture.

We bowed with newfound devotion and our hearts swelled with the joy of Divine love. That was the magic my soul looked for in all the mysteries of life. With an intuitive understanding, Karin looked into my eyes… I silently offered my heart to her soul.

Days later I remembered the long-forgotten story Dr. Jianyu told us about Narada and the cup of water. Coincidence, I wondered, or premonition. How I would like to meet Dr. Jianyu again.

After Karina's appearance with the angel, Karin started going deep in her meditations for lengthy periods. Watching her, she looked just like the yogis that came at night to the temple in the Himalayans and meditated motionless hour after hour, I could only imagine that she must have devoted many past lives to Yoga. Although I made a supreme effort, my wandering thoughts eluded my constant attempts at restraining them. Sometimes I had success, sometimes not, but Karin did not have to wage an inner war to find that complete inner peace.

It was the most arduous time of our lives yet became the most spiritually rewarding. Reflecting that sometimes an unfortunate or tragic event works as a stimulus to prod us on to a better understanding of ourselves and those that influence us, and the deeper meaning of life's intricacies.

22: THE MAGIC GARLAND

Fall arrived, and the changing colors of the trees painted the scenery wherever one looked. In the chilly evenings of October, Karin quietly sat in a rocking chair making colored beads of dough using fragrant herbs, and coloring extracts for the garlands that we would use for the Christmas tree. The potent extracts taken from wild berries were a gift from an Indian tribe in the southwest. The coloring needed careful handling; permanently staining anything it came in contact with. A painted clay pot filled to the brim of the beads rested by her side. Days passed as she rolled the dough slowly and tediously between her palms to make them nice and round.

During the holiday season, we always welcomed friends and acquaintances that visited with glassfuls of Karin's heavenly eggnog and her butter cookies. One afternoon a distant neighbor came with a friend named Alice, whose four-year-old child,

Daniel, had a severe liver problem from the time he was an infant. He was unresponsive to treatment and suffered from constant pain. He was a very likable boy but cried persistently.

"That is why I don't go out often," Alice bemoaned as she apologized for his crying.

Karin replied, "You have nothing to apologize for." We felt so bad for them both.

The young lady had few friends. We talked on, enjoying the eggnog when Karin realized the boy had been quiet for a long time. She took a quick look in the living room only to see Daniel eating to his delight a long strand of the beads. She shrieked and picked him up. He had devoured dozens of the beads. We all feared he would get violently ill. We did not know what to do.

Alice said, "Not to worry, I will keep a close eye on him through the night. It was not the first time he had eaten things he should not have. Children do that." They left, and we made countless prayers that night for the boy and continued daily.

Days passed, and we did not know how to contact Alice. Her friend that brought her here left to visit her parents. We were very anxious, feeling responsible for what happened, and kept praying for him.

The day after Halloween, a carriage arrived late in the afternoon. We looked out the window and what relief in our hearts to see Alice and Daniel.

Alice beamed, all smiles coming up the front veranda steps. Before even saying hello, Karin questioned, "How is Daniel?"

Alice just said, "Look."

His eyes were clear. When he first visited, they were dull and yellowish.

"Come inside and sit down. We were so worried about Daniel. What did you do?" asked Karin.

"Nothing, he had a little stomachache the night we left here, but by the next afternoon, he was well. A little over a week went by, and I realized he had not cried much all day and his eyes were clearing. And afterward, he got better and happier every day.

"Not only that, but I also had the first entire night's sleep in years. The first night it was a sensation indescribable. I feel like a new person, alive again."

After saying that, she just cried and cried with her forehead resting on the palms of her hands, as though she was letting the floodgate open from years of repressed emotions. It was so sad, yet so heartwarming. After she dried her eyes Karin asked, "Alice, but how?"

"That's just what I would like to know."

Alice then continued, "There is only one explanation and it could not have been the eggnog, although it was delicious, because Daniel did not drink any. I thought about it over and over; the beads for the Christmas tree."

"Could it be?" we wondered.

"It is the only explanation. What is in those beads?" Alice questioned.

"Well, I mixed herbs, flour, and wild berry extracts for coloring. It doesn't seem possible it could help."

"Karin during the years trying to treat Daniel I met many others with similar problems, would you mind if we tried some beads on one of them?"

"I don't mind, as long as there is no danger anybody could get sick from them."

"The responsibility will be mine. A person I know, Marc Desdeni, who works for the newspaper, has a daughter with a similar problem. We met at the doctors' office several times. He has already seen what it can do in Daniel's case and he is extremely interested in experimenting with it."

"Okay, I'll wrap some up for you, I have plenty. Perhaps the wild berry extracts have healing power. I guess she can take them with a cup of water. It might taste horrible."

"Karin, it doesn't matter as long as it works. This is exciting, and I cannot thank you enough. But it is getting dark already, and I should get going. As soon as I learn something, I will let you know."

After Alice left, Karin asked what I thought about the cure and I replied, "That I just did not know, but it would be wonderful if it worked."

Three weeks passed before we saw Alice again, our curiosity mounting every day. She arrived and looked youthful again. From Alice, we learned how a lack of sleep can wreck a person.

We sat on the porch as she recounted how Marc Desdeni tried giving doses to his daughter in numerous ways, nothing happened. He just remarked to me afterward, "That's the way it goes with things that are not scientific. There's nothing to it, don't waste your time."

Alice said, "It disappointed me, but I wasn't convinced they don't work, maybe he did something wrong."

"I don't see how he could go wrong," Karin replied.

"Anyway, I want to make one more test. It cannot hurt to try. It is for another girl I know, about fourteen years old. She does not live too far from me and has been under treatment for over a year from abdominal problems without any improvement. After what we have been through with doctors, you get to know other people who are suffering as well. Would you mind?"

"I don't mind at all if you want to. I'll wrap up another packet of the beads."

"Thanks, I am going there now. They are expecting me."

Karin and I also felt a little disappointed and figured Daniel would have healed anyway. Just a coincidence, Marc probably was right.

Thanksgiving arrived with freezing rain. We were always thankful for the abundance in our lives, but this Thanksgiving sadness took hold without Karina. Having lost, what we loved so much; the holiday ended up less than joyous.

The day Alice returned, I was out in the back, splitting wood. She told us, "Gracie, the young girl I wanted to help with the beads took them for over two weeks now. Nothing happened. I really can't understand it."

"Would do me a favor and bring Gracie here to visit. Just to stop by and say hi?" I asked Alice.

"Sure, I would be glad to, I'll pick her up and stop by a little later."

"Good, we'll see you then."

After she left Karin questioned me why I wanted to see Gracie. "Because I think it was you that healed Daniel, not the beads. What did you do after Alice and Daniel left that day when he ate the beads?"

"I prayed and prayed for him."

"Yes, we both did. But what is your idea of praying?"

"Well, I concentrated and visualized Daniel until I could see what was wrong with him. His liver did not look well." Then Karin went on explaining what she was doing, which no one taught her. It amazed me; she just knew. Her depth and power of visualization, and the technique she used, were well beyond my capabilities. In deep concentration, she could see with clarity a disease or an injury not visible to the naked eye. The ability came naturally to her. Not that it was easy for her; it took a taxing effort on her part. Karin never realized she had this ability until now and remained unconvinced.

"You healed Daniel, not the beads."

"But we both prayed day after day."

"Sorry, but I can't do what you are able to do."

"Well, if that is true why did I need to go to Dr. Jianyu when I was ill?"

"Did you try to heal yourself?"

"No."

"Even saints get sick too," I reminded her. "How many saints suffering from terrible afflictions continued on healing and curing others?"

"Yeah okay, but maybe it is all just coincidence, and he would have gotten better anyway."

"Yes, that is possible, but I do not think so, and that is why I asked Alice to bring Gracie here; that you could see her. Then if you are willing, we can see if my theory is correct"

"Do you think so?"

"Are you willing to find out?"

"All right, but please say nothing of your motive when Gracie comes here. I don't want her to have disappointing expectations again."

Later in the day, we met Gracie and as we sat on the steps watching the light snow falling, I asked her, "What's wrong?"

"The doctors for over a year now have tried to find an explanation and cure for terrible pains in my intestines. The last one wants to perform surgery and open me up to see what is wrong, but my father is against it and left that as a last case possibility. But time is running out, and I am scared. The doctor thinks it's appendicitis."

The subject dropped, and Karin served her special cream pie for the guests with lots of cookies in the living room by the Christmas tree. They were content.

Before they left, I took Alice on the side and asked, "Will you be able to stop by Gracie's house and see how she is doing in two weeks and let me know?"

"Sure, I would be glad to."

They left, and we went to the meditation room. When Karin finally arouse, I asked her, "Could you see anything wrong?"

"Yes, it is not the appendix. The problem is her uterus on the right side. What is wrong I do not know. I only know that something is not right there."

We both embarked on an attempt at curing Gracie. I tried and tried to do the same as Karin and could not, but even if what I did only added a tiny drop of help to her bucket, I would not give up.

A week later, Karin mentioned, "The uterus is getting clearer. I think it may be healing."

Every day thereafter it got clearer and brighter. Karin started to believe in herself a little. Although she thought it might be just her imagination playing with her.

Christmas was two weeks away, and we just arrived from the general store when a carriage came up the drive. It was Alice, and she was not alone.

"Hi, I brought Don and Betty, Gracie's mom and dad."

"You cannot imagine how happy we are," Betty said with a big smile.

"Gracie is no longer suffering. We don't know what you did. But less than a week after we left here, she began feeling better. Then every day better and better."

We spent the early afternoon in their company. Karin feeling at ease with them talked about the spiritual path and then told them, "We both made special prayers for her getting better and asked for God's blessings."

Betty remarked, "Your prayers work like nothing we have ever heard of before. We will be forever thankful to God and the both of you. We want to know how we can repay you?"

"Your happiness already has," answered Karin with a smile.

After they left, I questioned Karin, "Where does all your power come from?"

"I don't know; I just meditate as you do."

"Nothing else?"

"No, I just silently chant one of those mantras you taught me that you learned in the Himalayas. I also try to practice the presence as much as I can."

"The presence of God?"

Karin nodded her head affirmatively. "You told me a long time ago we should, so I do."

"You do this all the time?"

"Well, often." She was doing everything I should have been doing, and I never knew it.

Karin did nothing absentmindedly, everything with deep concentration. She became as if a dynamo of healing energy. I could only imagine that besides what she is doing now, her power of healing must have come from a past life or lives.

There is no way to describe the emptiness in our hearts when Christmas arrived. Karina's death was still so fresh in our minds. What joy in the past watching Karina opening presents and putting flowers next to a small statue of the Lord Jesus and decorating the Christmas tree. Not being good with encouraging words, I tried to console Karin anyway, "We should be very thankful for the joy Karina gave us and knowing the joy she is living now." She absentmindedly agreed but remained withdrawn and silent.

A little while later we thought we heard someone singing a Christmas carol. Could it be Sam and Ingrid were having a Christmas party? Curiosity got the best of us as we opened the door to look. To our disbelieving eyes, the entire circus crew surrounded the veranda. For a few moments we just silently looked at each other. Then smothered in hugs and showered with gifts, the tears flowed in an endless stream. What a celebration that followed. They brought every type of delectable treat imaginable. Everything prepared under the watchful eyes of Miss Maria. Their visit could only be the wondrous workings of God. Karin and I proffered silent prayers from our hearts.

They stayed for several days and told us how after we gave them all the equipment; they started a circus on their own. They wisely chose Miss Maria as the boss. A young group of gymnasts replaced the trapeze act. B Bob the clown took over the magic as best he could, and the rest stayed the same.

Miss Maria mentioned, "Those that recognized us as we traveled were heartbroken to hear of what happened. But anyway, we are holding our own. We want you to know that whenever you decide, you are welcome back to take the reins again."

We offered our appreciation but affirmed, "The circus days are over for us. It is wonderful to know that you all stayed together. That is the nicest gift you could have given us. We were so concerned over your wellbeing. When I left for Europe, I never realized the hardship it would create for all of you. Karin and I are so thankful you can't imagine."

"We too… we too."

23: THE JOURNALIST

The weather finally warmed for the January thaw on the 21st and stayed that way until early February. Most of the snow melted off the roads.

But for us, an unresolved question remained, where is the karma going that created the diseases Karin was curing? Is it burned up by the energy of the prayers and with God's blessing? Or is it just recoiling, getting ready to strike again at an opportune moment? Can it be that Karin is absorbing it all in herself? If only we had Okaala nearby to help and give us direction. We prayed constantly for Divine guidance that we do the right thing.

Finally, with me, the ability to visualize began to manifest and made it a little easier for Karin. I always thought healers worked like Dr. Jianyu, letting their healing power work through their hands in contact with the body. But with Karin, it was all mind power. Contact with someone else's body disturbed her powerful concentration from the vibrations she absorbed from them.

March brought with the brighter sunshine other healing challenges. Six months had passed since the first meeting with Alice. Karin was becoming known as a reclusive wonder-worker. Now almost every week someone new showed up at our door. The situation was getting a little scary for us. There is a limit to what one can do. But how do you say no to someone suffering?

Karin called me by her side as I approached the veranda, "Andrew, I have a problem. Remember Patricia, who had severe arthritis in her legs? The same symptoms started in my legs a week ago and it is getting worse. From the others, nothing has shown up. Maybe it is a coincidence and is something else unrelated, I just don't know."

"Karin, we need to stop until we understand all this better."

"Andrew, even with taking on the suffering of others it would be worthwhile if only they would wake up spiritually from the experience and it stimulated in them a desire to know God. They all professed eternal gratitude to God, and except for Alice, no one has come back to question how or remembered their promise to God. Not that I expected anything in return, I am so glad that I could help someone and serve God. But alas, it seems in vain to take on the burdens of another if in the end result nothing changes, nothing learned by it all."

"I know only too well what you are saying, and now it's becoming clearer why God so close; remains so silent, so eclipsed until our heart is truly open to Him. But looking at the bigger picture, perhaps you have planted a spiritual seed and someday it will sprout, maybe not even in this lifetime, but that doesn't matter."

"I guess you are right."

"Either way, we need to stop for a while and see what is happening with you and those who were healed. Tricked once before by Zenkai trying to help people, I will not let it happen again."

But it was too late. Our neighbors the Johnsons came over

with the weekly newspaper. A story about Karin made the front page. Written by Marc Desdeni, the journalist who was the first person Alice gave the beads to, that did nothing for his daughter. She was the only person whom Karin did not cure.

In bold letters, the story began.

WITCHCRAFT IN FAIRFIELD COUNTY

Someone recently asked me if I would like to try a cure for my young daughter of her persistent illness. The magical home-made medicine cured her son of an apparently incurable disease. Being open-minded and trusting, I tried it on my child. The strange brightly colored pills did nothing, absolutely nothing.

Recently I have heard more claims of this woman curing people of the incurable. If these reports are all true and it is not the useless magic medicine I tried, there can only be one answer and you can decide for yourself.

The person who gave me the medicine told me that the woman who made it worships Shiva. He is the Indian God of death and destruction. How could someone worshipping death make a cure, it is contradictory? To look at a picture of Shiva is frightening; he appears as the embodiment of evil. He sits with a threatening trident by his side, and deadly cobras around his arms, ready to kill at his will. Next to him sits a demonic woman. The scene is full of inexplicable horrors and strange magical things; black magical to be sure.

If there was a cure, it could only have been with the help of these fiendish beings. Is it Witchcraft or Charlatanism? Hopefully, it is just Charlatanism. But from the looks of things, I can only draw one conclusion.

His description was not that of the beautiful, loving, and benevolent Shiva we knew. The distorted reporting would have frightened even us if we did not know better. What he referred to as the demonic woman is Kali, the Mother of creation. Where he found the illustration, I cannot imagine. Alice in her zeal must have talked too much, too poorly understood.

The reporter did not realize that Shiva dematerializes suffering, and old decaying forms of life that they can reincarnate into new youthful forms, full of energy and vitality. The cobras represent various aspects of creation, as well as the energy of the body's powerful life forces. All the other images around Shiva are spiritually symbolic.

Karin was in a state of shock. We both knew not only would we suffer, but all those that she healed and their families. Marc Desdeni knew putting the fear of witchcraft in the minds of the readers would get him noticed. Not caring whom he was hurting to make a name for himself. He also knew no one would ever be foolish enough to step forward in our defense.

To defend ourselves would only spread the story even more. And if a big newspaper noticed the story, we would have no place in the country to have peace again. It could set a wave of destruction snowballing in the lives of all we recently touched.

"The good, will always win out, always," I reassured Karin. But at what cost, I wondered as doubts assailed my mind. We decided to go to Pennsylvania, where my father left me his farmhouse when he died. In our travels with the circus, we always stopped there for a rest. It was just outside Lancaster, close by the Amish people. They were a people more akin to our ways, although with different precepts.

That very night, with the Johnsons help, we packed up the large wagon with all we could fit in. There was just no time to dwell on a solution. Once the witchcraft ball gets rolling, you never know where it will end. We could only hope the people that read the story would just pass it off as an unfounded exaggeration.

Luckily, Alice and the journalist knew nothing of our circus

past. Not even our last name.
We were in New York by late afternoon.

24: THE INN

E arly evening, we stopped at an Inn. Saying nothing to Karin, but again I am like a fugitive running like a hunted criminal.

The next day riding along I wondered, should I have had the courage to stay back home and stand up for what I believe. Running from England and now from Connecticut. But no, I concluded, I would not take the chance and let anyone harm Karin in any form. It was not a lack of courage. Or then again, am I just making an excuse for myself?

Hours passed as I absentmindedly drove the carriage on the bumpy road, but my doubt remained unresolved. What is it with the spiritual life and me, I reflected over and over?

The sun had just set on our fifth day of travel when we arrived at an Inn in Pennsylvania that was part of a large dairy farm.

In the evening we went downstairs to enjoy the warmth of the fireplace. A lively discussion was taking place with the guests and what appeared to be two Brothers from a Monastery sitting with them. The Brothers were wearing heavy robes, and one had a large cross hanging around his neck.

"The last thing in the world I need right now is a sermon, do you want to go back upstairs," I questioned Karin?

"No, I want to warm up." We quietly joined the group.

One of the Brothers was in the middle of making a point. "The universe is in a harmonious flux of continuous evolving change. Chaos does not exist in Nature undisturbed by man or in man undisturbed by himself. Even when disturbed, both man and Nature tend to self-compensate.

"The problem with chaos is in our perception. Often as we try to do only good it seems all that happens to us goes bad no matter how hard we try.

"Then we see another person who constantly does terrible things and seemingly never tries to be good and continually attracts wealth and enjoyable things."

I silently wondered if he was talking to Karin and me.

"But chaotic it is not; it all evolves from the karma we talked about earlier this evening. Good karma is like stored up fuel that keeps the lantern of success healthy and bright. Abusing your abundance and living a life of greed and evil ways; one day when you least expect it your barrel of abundance will run dry, the lamp of success and health will flicker and go out. Keep the barrel full of well thought out good intentions in all you do.

"It is the perception of our mind and how it responds to the stimulus which it is given that creates a vision of harmony or chaos. That is to say, we interpret our environment by how we perceive it."

One of the Brothers walked behind where we were sitting, where the light was a little dimmer. He reached into a deep pocket in his woolen robe and took out a folded picture. He opened it and asked us, "What is this picture of?" Everyone agreed it was a picture of a lovely saint.

He then went back by the fireplace and held the picture close to a bright lantern and called us, "Come close and take another look." Her face was washed out in places and darkened in others, fissures and hairline cracks passed through the picture, many tiny holes perforated the image.

He then asked, "Is she a lovely saint or is she a distorted nondescript woman?" No one answered. He continued, "An analytical person will look closely and with intelligence describe the cracks and fissures. A person of spiritual perception will also perceive this, and at the same time see the harmonious essence and a wonderful aura of translucent light that surrounds and emanates from the image.

"So, what have we seen? At a distance, with our physical eyes, we saw a lovely saint. Close up analytically we saw chaos. Penetrating deeper with spiritual vision, we discover a wondrous essence. It all comes down to perception.

"And that is the problem with life. We are too close to it. We either must step back and see it as a lovely saint or delve into it and discover the spiritual essence. Both would be best.

"That is not to say the dualities do not exist - pain hurts and pleasure pleases - a hot bath, a cold bath. But with the proper perception, we see life as the lovely saint with a spiritual aura.

"On the other hand, mistaken perceptions lead to misconceptions: misconceptions between people – between countries – between religions. The result is what?"

Everyone answered, "Chaos."

"Exactly… but when the mind is still and concentrated, we perceive Nature as harmonious and endlessly intriguing. Remember the biblical words, *Be still and know that I am God* (Psalms 46:10)."

Someone then remarked, "That's all nice, but in real life when one tries and tries to be successful and nothing goes right, how can one have a positive perception? To him, the world is nothing but chaotic."

"Yes, that is true. Try as you will, you will probably not paint like a Michael Angelo nor write like Shakespeare unless your karma from the past has led you to develop those abilities and they now flourish in your life. These abilities took perhaps many incarnations to develop. But nothing is impossible with enough will power.

"The difficulty is you just don't know your entire past and where you are at this point, and maybe you will be the next Michael Angelo or Shakespeare if that is what you so desire. For you may already have the seeds of brilliant success to be an artist, architect, or a scientist ready to sprout and do not know it. With all your wisdom, strength, and energy water the seeds of success, then cultivate them into reality. Give it your best at being successful. Even if success does not come at once, it will set in motion the karmic wheels that will make it happen, but in God's time.

"The true key to success is just doing your absolute best and praying to God to guide you in all that you do. Being 'Still' and praying deeply day by day. Then use all your energy, strength, and willpower to see in your mind's eye the fruition of that dream. Then you will know that whatever materializes in your life will bring inner peace. That is the Key for true success. For how many wealthy people suffer as much as a poor hungry person, although their reasons may be different? Not that extremes make one suffer. Many poor and wealthy people are happy and content. True success can only then can be measured by the lasting inner peace it brings. Not just the fleeting happiness and joy wealth can sometimes bring.

"Is success only to have a big bank account, or is success lasting inner peace and joy?"

The guests light-heartedly voiced their varied opinions.

The Brother then continued, "The wise can have both who don't forget patience and that it is all in God's time. Do not be disappointed and do not give up if success does not materialize in your perception of time and be very content if it does. And the same goes for everything else.

"Past, present, and the resultant karmic fate are not engraved in granite like a gravestone. But a stream of continuous input and output of all our thoughts and deeds, like a multitude of tributaries feeding an ever-changing river, creating for the future what will appear as happenstance, only because we have forgotten the past. But always remember we are the weavers of what we wear. Thus, we can change our destiny.

"That is one beautiful aspect of Creation: Nothing, but nothing is impossible to accomplish.

"Never despair when difficulty knocks at your door. The forces of negativity are always ready to strike and impede your efforts when you least expect it.

"'Be Still,' sit and pray with deep concentration… And?

"Yes, ask God to guide you.

"Make the effort every day to go beyond chaotic perceptions of this world and discover for yourself the true harmonious essence of all, God."

"But how can He be the essence of all, it's extremely hard to imagine?" One questioned.

"At night In Dreams, we create friends and enemies, lovely scenes, and nightmarish ghouls. We visit distant places with just a thought. We create homes and factories, fires, and babies. Infinite is our creative power. And during the dream, everything is so real, pain and pleasure, the bite of a snake, the kiss of a lover. All you create is inseparable from your consciousness. You are unbrokenly aware of all that you create and with a wisp of your thought a world disappears, or another is born.

"That is what God does, He dreams into existence the flowers and trees, the moon and sky, you, and me, and that is why you are inseparable from Him.

From His thoughts,

From His awareness,

From His creation."

"Dreamed all into existence?" another quizzically questioned.

"The Masters say you can bake a cake in the kitchen and leave it on the table, but you are not inseparably part of the cake. When you walk into another room and forget about the cake, it is still there. But when you dream of a cake, you are irreversibly part of that cake. You can make it any flavor or color, sweet or tart, chocolate, or vanilla, but when the dream ends so does the cake. We are in an infinite, never-ending dream of God.

"But unlike our dreams, He gives those in His dream creation free will… to do good or bad creating good or evil karma. And He does not choose favorites, giving more to some and less to others.

"But He also allows distorting shadows of Maya to enter the dream that conceals our real Nature so that by trials we can learn to be like Him, even when surrounded by diversity and adversity."

"Okay, but why is it so hard to find inner peace and lasting happiness," the same guest asked?

"Our desires bind us to the material world with all its undulations of happiness-pain, joy-sorrow, hot-cold, sickness-health created by the dualities of Maya.

"Inner peace comes, and peace goes, it is very slippery. The only thing that will bring peace lasting, unyielding, unending is God."

"Why? Another guest questioned."

"Your transcendental home in Him has long been forgotten in your memory. But your soul has not forgotten, as your desires lead you on a blindfolded journey back home; while you try to find joy in a new carriage, delicious food, or in lovemaking, the list is endless. But fulfilled desires are ever unfruitful, never producing more than just temporary satisfaction before new desires take hold in an endless circle. For everything that exists in the material world is in a constant state of change. Nothing is what it was a moment ago. Not you, not the sun, not the shimmering dew.

"You can only find unending, ever new peace and joy by returning home to the One that dreamed all into existence. All the great saints say His nature is ever new, infinite bliss, ever existing."

The guests, in deep introspection, left one by one, as they thanked the Brothers and retired.

Karin and I remained with the Brothers. We all turned our silent gaze to the fireplace. Sitting still with the devout company, we felt as though at the feet of Moses on top of Mt. Sinai, as the leaping flames engulfed our minds.

The frustrations of the last days lost their grip. We slept peacefully that night.

Ambrosial delight is the only way to describe the breakfast with pancakes and freshly made butter, doused with maple syrup. It brought back fond memories for me of Pierre, the chef on Kitty's ship, a wonderful breakfast after a trying time of difficulty.

25: LANCASTER

Sadly, the brothers left before we awoke in the morning. We never learned what order they belonged to but being with them the previous evening was just what we needed. Karin and I became talkative again. Traveling long distances in the late winter presented a constant danger, never knowing when a snowstorm could arrive. We felt secure knowing the roads well and where we could stop for the night. But it took ten days of hard traveling before we arrived in Lancaster, and fortunately, it did not snow. The house needed a good cleaning but was in decent shape with plenty of firewood in the shack.

We had friends and acquaintances here in Lancaster, which brought tranquility to our situation. It was our home away from home and luckily stayed that way. Keeping busy getting the property in order kept our minds temporarily off the inner turmoil. However, our being in Lancaster became a constant reminder that life's tests just do not go away for us.

Torment had become a faithful companion in our life. Although we would have preferred other company, it functioned as a driving force to break the bonds of earthly attachments. It forced us deeper into our spiritual pursuit.

Fortunately, we had a better understanding than most. But even so, God's ways can appear inexplicable and difficult to accept when hardship arrives. We tried to accept that is what faith is all about.

We bought the newspaper from New York whenever we found one. But discovered nothing related to Marc Desdeni's story. I felt relieved that by the end of March Karin's legs felt better. She did not try healing herself as she did for others. But I prayed for her constantly. The cold frames by the shack were already full of young sprouting vegetable and flower plants. Hearing ducks quacking away by the gurgling stream that traversed the backside of the property, I went to watch and sat on a fallen log.

My mind wandered, remembering Okaala asking me to be an example to attract others to the transforming power of meditation. Thinking I would have been the source for hundreds turning to Yoga. But that was not in God's plan. What have I accomplished? Not one person have I inspired, besides Karin and Karina. Then again, perhaps that was my only purpose, to relight their interest in this life. If that is the case, then it was worth it all. Whether spectators or coworkers, no one that knew them could imagine that hidden behind their sweet smiles were two saintly souls.

The months passed, and the bright sun warmed the cool morning air in early October as I fixed the broken fence posts. Hearing a carriage approaching, I walked around to the roadside. Could it be Nantu, with Sam Johnson, our neighbor from Connecticut?

My heart pounding fast, I ran over and hugged Nantu. Sam gave a cordial handshake. Karin watched the spectacle from the porch. But remained apprehensive, not knowing what news Sam brought, or the motive of Nantu's arrival. She too gave Nantu a warm, welcoming embrace. Karin did not question Sam about the news. We walked around the property reminiscing as Karin prepared food.

After dinner, Sam told us, "The entire witchcraft issue never materialized. The story was so exaggerated that everyone passed it off as sensationalism. If it were years ago, he would have been a hit with the fanatics. But now, with the death and destruction of the Civil War, people are terrified of what the future will bring. Their children are dying down south.

"The last thing anyone wanted was more disturbing news. His imaginative story was trifling compared to the reality of the growing obituary pages. A gruesome toll of death grew daily from the war. Unbelievable as it seemed, they confirmed over two-hundred thousand soldiers are dead already.

"That reporter with your story ended up looking like a fool. Nobody gave the least attention to the story, except those with parentage from India. A well-written letter to the editor published two weeks later came from one of them. It explained beautifully about Shiva and Kali. Kind of the things you had already told me. It was a relief to read the story. It gave me the impression that it was the newspaper's way of giving an apology. I saved the paper for you, but in the haste of coming here I forgot it."

"That is great news. I'm so glad you are both here."

"Alice visited many times looking for you. She was heartbroken. You saved her son, and she felt she destroyed your life. Anyway, if you come back it will be as if nothing ever happened."

"Please tell Alice we know that she did everything out of her heart. We wish everyone could be like her."

Sam went out for a long walk, looking around the distant farmhouses. Karin and I were alone with Nantu in the living room.

"If it weren't for Sam, I never would have found you again," remarked Nantu.

"What in the world brought you here?"

"After all you have been through, I know you will not want to hear more disheartening news, but there are problems in China, and they are affecting her neighbors.

"Earlier in the century, British merchants began smuggling opium into China to balance their purchases of tea for export to Britain. It created addiction in incredible proportions throughout the country. To put an end to opium's wanton destruction of human life, in 1839 China enforced its prohibitions on the importation of opium by destroying opium in Canton, that they confiscated from British merchants. Great Britain, which had been looking to end China's restrictions on foreign trade, responded by attacking Chinese coastal cities. China, unable to withstand modern arms, fell defeated. Two years later, with no alternative, they signed the Treaty of Nanjing.

"History repeated itself and the second opium war started several years ago between China and a British-French alliance demanding the legalization of opium.

"In the meantime, to make matters worse, over ten years ago Hong Xiuquan started the Taiping rebellion. The leader formally declared the establishment of the Heavenly Kingdom of Peace with himself as absolute ruler. He considered himself the son of Jesus. The Taiping rebellion proclaimed itself as a Christian uprising against the Manchu oppressors. The army formed mostly of miners in its beginnings. They proved to be clever fighters with their simple weapons.

"This army defeated well protected walled in cities by digging not one tunnel, but two tunnels under the fortresses. They would let the warriors inside the city discover one of the tunnels, and when they entered the tunnel to attack, the miners blew it up. They then entered the city from the second tunnel.

"And there is much more, massive flooding, then drought and famines. Untold millions have died already in these years.

"Until recently the mountainous areas of Tibet and the eastern borders of India haven't suffered from all the conflict and Nature's upheavals. However, small roving bands from the Taiping armies have been going greater distances searching out food and anything of a monetary value to sustain their rebellion.

"A little over a year ago, our fields in the distant lower valley on the Tibetan side were attacked. They took all our recently harvested grains. They left nothing. No one resisted, and they did not kill anyone. But when I left to come here eight months ago, the grain supplies dwindled to where the hungry villagers began sacrificing valuable Yaks. It was difficult to decide how much of the grains to eat, and how much to save for planting. We had no way to buy seeds. We take what edibles we can from the lower plain, but the quantity is negligible, and the need is great. And it is not just our village. Soon the weak will start dying. The situation is critical."

But Nantu, "What can I do?"

"Can I be direct and honest?"

"Yes, stop with the formalities."

"We need money for wheat, rice, millet, and barley to eat, and to plant. We have no one else to ask for help."

"How much do you need?"

"As much as you can spare. Talk it over with Karin and let me know what you both decide."

As we spoke Karin became unaware of the conversation, immersed in a vision as an ominous black cloud filled the house. She could not understand the significance. The cloud slowly dissipated as Nantu asked, "Karin, can I make some tea for you?" Oblivious, she did not answer.

I then repeated the question, "Karin, would you like Nantu to make some tea?"

"Oh, sorry, I was a little distracted. Who would not want

some of Nantu's delicious tea? Those oriental teas are so wonderful."

While Nantu made tea in the kitchen, I spoke to Karin about Nantu's request for money. She replied, "It is all up to you, whatever you decide."

"It is so hard to know; we planned our retirement expenses so well. If I say no to Nantu, it is like I am killing them. If I say yes, it may create a lot of financial hardship for us in the coming years."

Delicious aromas accompanied Nantu into the living room as we spent the afternoon reminiscing. He told me how he travelled by steamers to get to the United States and was able to pay his way working on the ships, mostly by shoveling coal into the steam engine's furnace. Not an easy task, and that is why it took so long to get here.

Alone in our room that evening, we discussed how much we could afford to give Nantu. Karin noted, "If things get tight, we can always sell one of the houses. We don't need them both." We decided we would give half of our savings and hoped it would be enough.

The next morning, after breakfast we sat with Nantu. Sam Johnson had already left with the carriage to view the Amish countryside. "Nantu we have about $5,000 – $6,000 we can give you for your traveling expenses and the grains. Will that suffice?"

"It is hard to know because they base the value of everything with silver and gold in China. It is too far to travel from the village to the Indian side of the mountain to buy grains. But I have been making calculations in my head. They sell grains by a picul, which is about 130 pounds and costs about 4 teals. One teal is about 40 grams of silver. And one dollar buys about 24 grams of silver. Therefore, every picul will cost about $6.70. But I need to check all this out again."

"Nantu, is it enough?"

"Yes, it is a blessing that will save a lot of lives and prevent a lot of suffering. It will buy a lot of grains."

26: VOYAGERS

Nantu, if it is all right with Sam, we can leave today for Connecticut and I will take the money out of the bank for you. Will you be leaving from New York or Boston?

"Well Oswell, that's another little detail."

"What do you mean... detail?"

"I was hoping you would return with me."

Karin turned pale as she instantly understood the foreboding significance of the black cloud the day before but mentioned nothing.

Okaala told me, "If you were kind enough to help financially, it would be safer traveling if you returned with me."

I would have felt warmer if Nantu had thrown me in an icy river, I swore I would never sail the seas again. And separated from Karin was unthinkable. My mind was in turmoil.

Nantu, "I will not leave Karin."

"But it is only temporary."

Nantu, "It doesn't matter; I will not leave Karin for anything of this world. I will not let her suffer again like I did last time."

"Oswell, it is not of this world, it is for God. He is also suffering in all those hungry souls and without your help, our villagers will be next to die of famine."

"Why oh why does He let this suffering go on relentlessly?"

"Maya and karma, you understand, don't you?"

"Yes, and no."

"Without the prod of suffering no soul would attempt to go beyond the realms of Divine Mother's creation to find the everlasting bliss of God-consciousness."

"Excellent Nantu, then why take away the evolutionary prod that is making souls move forward?"

"Because it is an integral part of the soul's higher evolution: learning how to work as God, angels, yogis, and saints do spreading their goodness on a sometimes not understanding humanity to minimize the dreadful karmic boomerang of negative thoughts, deeds, and actions. The suffering would be a lot worse without their help, as well as all the helping prayers from humankind wherever they are."

I clasped Karin's palm on my forehead saying, "This is just not happening."

She said nothing. She did not need to. Her tears said it all.

Nantu continued, "When we travel back to the village, we will travel mostly through India, and being with an American we will have no problems with the authorities. Once there our travels will be near the Tibet border and being that I am Chinese we will have no problems with them either."

Sam returned and noted the gloom of the somber atmosphere and went without a word to his room. Karin went to our bedroom. She knew we would be separated for a long time again. The approaching loneliness was already taking its toll.

She lied down, staring aimlessly at the ceiling.

I sat by her side, but I found no words of solace to offer. I quietly left the room.

The only positive aspect for us in this whole scenario became clear. She would be safe here, alone amongst the Amish. Even with the Johnsons nearby, I would not have felt as secure leaving her alone in Connecticut. There is just a different serenity here. It just somehow felt this is where we needed to be. As I sat, Nantu motioned for me to go outside.

Far from the bedroom, he commented, "We cannot delay too long, every day is crucial. We need to get there by April to plant the barley, wheat, and other grains, or we will miss another harvest. It will be a long trip and we have lots to do before the voyage."

"Nantu, I will wait for her consent."

"I understand. In the meantime, I will go to the market with Sam and get what I need to make food for this week's traveling."

I was standing in the back doorway looking towards the garden when the old grandfather clock struck noon with its reassuring gongs. Karin soon approached and locked her swollen loving eyes on mine without blinking for a long time then finally spoke, "If I lived in the village with a child dying of hunger and knew there was someone that could save us and didn't because it was inconvenient; that would be even more painful than the tortuous suffering of slowly dying. It is a blessing we can help. I wish it could be another way, any other way."

She put her head on my chest as she repeated, "We will be together soon, we will be together soon."

"Why don't you come with us?"

"I would love to see the Himalayans and the magnificent temples in India and visit Tibet, but not now. I will stay here; I won't go back to Connecticut without you either."

Karin packed my clothes before Nantu, and Sam returned. Nantu prepared lunch and food for our travels. The evening passed quietly, Karin and I retired early. Our precious last hours together.

By sunrise, we had already left Lancaster behind. The roads were rough after an early frost. Two days later we lost a day of traveling with a broken wheel. Sam had a spare, but it took an entire day to get the broken one fixed.

That night we stopped at a quaint Inn to stay for the night. Entering the front hall was shocking. Instead of people traveling, visiting, or doing business as I expected, it was full of wounded Union soldiers returning home from the battlefield, some moaning in pain. They survived the battle on the field from rifle shots and bayonets. Now they were fighting another agonizing battle trying to save their lives. Their sunken eyes and grief-stricken faces could best describe what war is firsthand.

It quickly drew me back to the vision I had in the Himalayas with Okaala and the scene where Ran Baja was describing the world as Hades.

I then toyed with the idea to do magic to lighten up the misery. But it seemed out of place and I did not know what to do, so I did nothing. The soldiers never parted with their iron cold rifles. The burnt black powder had the aroma of death.

We arrived at my home in Connecticut eight days later and went to the bank and took out $8,500. A third more than I had planned. $5,000 -$6,000 for the village, enough for the trip back and forth, and $1,000 I would send to Karin. I asked Sam to bring it to her by early Spring. Our life saving was evaporating. I had planned move our bank account to Lancaster after the winter, but now it will have to wait until I return from my travels.

I asked Sam to bring us to New York, but I would have liked to have sailed from Boston. We needed to get silver and or gold to trade for the grains and seeds in China and India. In New York, I knew a place to do this safely. It would be a shorter trip for Sam. I went up to the loft in the barn with Nantu and he helped me lower a large trunk. It was one of the few things I had left from the circus. It had ingenious secret panels. We would use it to hide the silver and gold on our travels.

Arriving in New York we ended up buying more gold than silver, to keep the weight and volume down. Arriving at the port we found a ship headed for England in two days. It was a new British steamship. Nantu would now have the pleasure to travel as a passenger.

Saying nothing to Nantu, but the destination put a knot in my stomach. Heading for Southampton, England. The last place in the world I wanted to go, so close to the Colonel and Lillian Blake. It was also Kitty's home port. Years had already passed, but I felt more at ease letting my hair and beard grow during the transatlantic trip.

This time we decided to go to Egypt and then travel by land through Suez to the Red Sea. The construction of the Suez Canal was still unfinished. Even so it would cut our travel time down by at least a month.

After arriving in Southampton, it only took three weeks to find a steamer going to Suez. After crossing Suez by land, we boarded another ship on the Red Sea headed for the Bay of Bengal a week later.

Almost three months passed before we arrived at the Bay of Bengal. From there we started our upstream travels from the Ganges River to Brahmaputra River. We were retracing our past steps of my first visit.

Before leaving Nantu went to a foundry where they make bronze statues and bought an armful of simple saintly ones with a hollow core. He came back to the hotel and filled them with the packets of gold and silver. I planned to leave my trunk with the hidden compartments at the hotel until my return trip home. He then closed the openings at the base of the statues with wooden plugs pushed in about one-half of an inch.

I accompanied him as he returned to the foundry. He asked them to pour molten bronze to seal the wood plugs, which they did without question. He sanded and polished the rough surface and the statues looked and felt like they were solid bronze and looked cheap enough not to attract any attention. The next day we left the hotel and continued our travels.

27: OKAALA

Without too many setbacks, Nantu calculated we could arrive at the village in early April when we would plant the barley and other grains. Our travels seemed blessed without incident.

The heat was oppressive in early February and without the normally heavy rain as we steamed up the Brahmaputra river. But unlike the unchanging view of the ocean voyage, the scenery, sights, and the local flotillas were ever-changing and fascinating. Boredom was a stranger here.

Arriving in Dibrugarh, the steamer trip ended. From here on in we would go back and forth between a carriage and simpler boats until we reached the deeper gorges where we would travel mostly with yaks. Nantu knew the closest point to the village where we could buy grains and seeds to take with us that could give the villagers immediate help. The outpost was not too distant. We slept in an Inn that night. For the rest of our travels, we would stay in improvised shelters.

We traveled on by a small boat for three days. Arriving at the outpost, our river traveling ended. We found a Sherpa with 12 yaks that we could use for our travels. With the twelve of them, we could carry about 1,800 lbs. He also would go with us to care for them. We bought 1,400 lbs. of wheat, barley, and rice for cooking and another 300 pounds for planting and miscellaneous items. We would have liked to have taken more, but at least it was an immediate temporary solution, while they planted the seeds. The villagers would also have money to buy more grains, seeds, and provisions.

The traveling was painstakingly slow, but as expected. Arriving at the top of a huge steep gorge with a breathtaking view, Nantu gestured, "Look over at that mountain peak, legend says that is the land of Shangri-La."

"Do you know anyone who has seen it?"

"No, only yogis with the power over Nature are courageous enough to travel those dense forests. Filled with tigers and snakes of every kind. There are dangers wherever you turn. And if they found Shangri-La, I don't think they would want to spoil it by telling anyone."

We left Shangri-La behind and continued our climb in the ever-steeper Himalayans, heading towards the Tibetan-India border.

Now higher up in the mountains, the trail steepened, and we went ever so slow in the rarified air, but the Sherpa knew how to pace the climb.

It was the middle of April when in the distance the village came into view. Crossing a narrow passage around a ledge, my knees suddenly got weak when I remembered my accident. Breathing heavily, I rested on a rock, and my composure returned.

Before we reached our destination, the villagers came out to greet us and help. It was saddening to see their happiness expressed with such emaciated smiles. I do not know how they had the strength to walk. This time they welcomed me like a long-lost hero. Nantu and I joined in the cooking festivities that day. They all ate to their heart's content.

In the evening I visited Master Okaala. Welcoming me at the open door, I bowed down with my hands and head touching his feet. It was just spontaneous and seemed the natural thing to do, not like something I should ceremoniously do.

This time he received me as a friend. He made me feel at home. I then questioned him how it was possible that the villagers had to suffer, living such peaceful and spiritual lives.

He responded, "Being part of the world we too share in its karma, good and bad. What affects the one affects the whole in one form or another. Although living spiritual lives now, the past lives of those that live here also have their accumulated multifarious karma to deal with."

"I imagined just the fact they lived here that they finished their karmic problems."

"God's way of teaching is not our way. You are trying to fathom the unfathomable. Just do all with undaunted courage, strength, and pure faith. You will wonder no longer when Divine Awakening in the Cosmic Consciousness of Samadhi comes upon you."

Exhausted from our travels, Nantu and I left after our warm welcome.

The next morning Nantu woke me early and commented, "They are taking food to other villages that are in the same situation as we are and would like your permission to give them some money. They have already done what is possible to help each other. We must now do what we can for them."

"Nantu, you know best what to do with the money. Use it how you feel will accomplish the most good."

"Okay, then I will let Okaala decide."

After a simple lunch, we arrived at the door of Atulya's residence by the Temple. He cordially invited us in. He looked at me with his intense eyes, now a young man. Still looking into my gaze, he then continued, "I am so pleased you have returned. Making the effort to come here and giving freely without expecting adulation or anything in return is the purest gift one can offer, for it is God's way. In silence He gives the whole Cosmos - every soul, every gram of gold, the sparkling sun, the reclusive moon, the grains, the plains, the clouds, and rain. He gives lover and friend, milk and cheese and a myriad of things that please - asking nothing in return.

"He gives and gives and patiently waits for the day one says, 'Heavenly Father I'm coming home, please show me the way.' Oswell you have done what few worldly men have accomplished. For your selfless giving, expecting nothing in return, and your spiritual progress, you and those close to you will reap many blessings into the distant future."

As he spoke, I reached into my pocket and offered him the moonstone dragon he gave me years ago. He accepted the dragon while holding my hand and remarked, "It has served its purpose." I never really understood its significance. The dragon remained a mystery for me, and Atulya did not seem anxious to explain. We spent an enlightening afternoon with him, a rare occasion speaking with him at length.

The village bordered the Tibetan - Indian frontier. They farmed in a distant lower valley on the Tibetan side. After resting for a day, I accompanied Nantu to the fields down below. Descending the barren mountain top to the lush valley below one could see tier after tier wonderfully engineered vegetable gardens; as well as the fields where wheat, barley, and other grains had adorned the valley before the Taiping raid.

The Taiping rebellion was losing force and ending. Except for a few roving bands on horseback stealing food and anything that could finance their war, the conflicts stayed far to the east in central China.

Now with seeds in hand, the villagers were planting every-where along the slopes and the lower valley. All were in high spirits. After several days of sight-seeing, we returned to the Vil-lage, another lengthy uphill journey.

This was such a joyous time for me. Karin was so right about coming here. Day after day throughout the travels she continu-ously remained in the background of my mind. Whether she felt sad or glad, I just intuitively knew. She was always just so close it seemed I could reach out and touch her presence.

The villagers were looking like their old healthy selves again. Several months passed, and the time to harvest approached. I had promised to help with the harvest and then finally return to Karin.

28: MOTHER NATURE'S HARVEST

It was late August when the early harvesting began. Vegetables growing on the slopes were abundant. The sun shone brightly as we gathered barley in the pristine valley. The barley and grains hauled up the mountain by Yaks. It was a lengthy process over the next two months, as the Yaks could take just so much each trip. A group of us went back up to the village with the first supply of grains. It was early December when Nantu and I went down with the final supply trip. The sun shone brightly in the pristine valley as we packed the last of the grains from the storage building.

From nowhere a band of Taiping warriors came galloping with swords flashing. We only had wooden poles to defend ourselves. The horsemen grouped in a tight pack headed towards Nantu. He grabbed the end of a long rope tied to a nearby post as they charged in his direction. At the last moment, he somersaulted to the side, and with all his force pulled the rope tight. It caught the first horses at knee height, and they went tumbling head over heels, and those behind trampled those in front before falling. With a pole, he took out one after the other that survived the crushing pile-up of horse and man. He kept the pole spinning with invisible speed. Another small group headed full speed towards us. Nantu threw me a sword from a slain horseman. The first horseman passed and slashed my arm. The second horseman leaned low to finish me, but my sword got the best of him. It all happened so fast.

......With a display of undaunted courage, Oswell fought on.

Back in Lancaster, Karin was in the garden with a small basket of apples feeding deer and their fawns their daily treat. It had become a ritual.

Suddenly there was a loud explosion… a misguided bullet from a hunter's rifle struck Karin. Realizing what he had done, the terrified hunter ran off. Karin's body fell to the frozen ground as blood flowed in a steady stream from her breast. Light snow fell and covered her.

At that same moment, Oswell froze for an instant, oblivious to all around him, as he watched a black cloud envelope the joyous countenance of Karin. Unheard a horseman with lightning speed silently approached him from behind with a blinding flash of his sword…. Nantu mercilessly killed the lone remaining demon on horseback.

Somber victory reigned as Nantu knelt over Andrew Ellison Oswell's lifeless form. Just crying over and over, "Oh God, why?"

Okaala presided over a special service for Oswell. True to his nature, the words short and terse:

"Andrew Ellison Oswell, a friend to all that knew him. A courageous man and an example for us all. He truly was 'The

Great Oswell.' May God and the Great Ones bless you always, our prayers are with you."

Atulya laid the moonstone dragon on top of his ashes. The ashes enshrined by the Temple.

They put a portion in a delicately carved vase for Nantu to bring to Karin. Okaala only mentioned, "She will be waiting and needs your help, I know it's a long arduous trip, but please go now."

While traveling, Nantu thought of a thousand different ways of what to tell Karin on meeting her but could not find the right words.

He arrived at the Lancaster home with the vase of Oswell's ashes. It was a cloudy early spring day, late afternoon. Over a year had passed since he last saw Karin. No one answered the front door. Walking around to the back, he found the door ajar. He called out for Karin, but still no answer. Nantu went inside. The house appeared disheveled and with no one around. On the kitchen table, he saw a tea-stained sheet of paper held in place by a cup, on which Karin had been writing. He read aloud,

Daily I grasped at the rays of the rising sun.

Dream rays of hope, accomplishment, everlasting serenity, and joy.

Holding them tight through the day, but alas a fruitless task as the night dissolved the light.

I awoke today and questioned why the delusive rays and not the Sun itself.

I bowed in the infinite heart of the Sun,

Where no enchanting rays of light's creation dare enter, to disturb the softly folding aura of endless bliss.

The Sun shall set no more,
Behind the luminous door.

SHE FOUND GOD!

Overwhelming happiness stole over Nantu, realizing what Karin had accomplished. Now ever free to fly the Celestial Sky.
He sat down, just staring at her words.
Turning the paper over, he read to himself the one sentence she had written on the backside:

Karina's eyes sparkled and seemed to say, I will be with you soon.

At the import of her words, his elation crashed like a shattered vase. Nantu suddenly realized why the disheveled house and the door ajar. He ran out to the garden and found Karin's frozen, blood-stained body lying half-exposed in the melting snow.

He kneeled over her and cried again and again, "Oh God, what have I done?" Hours passed as the sun dimmed and darkness reigned in the moonless night, Nantu's head motionless on her lifeless form.

Distracted by light, Nantu lifted his head. The brilliant glow of Shiva sitting in the lotus posture illumined the night. By his side sat Karin, Oswell, and Karina, the astral setting indescribably beautiful. Unspoken love flowed unspoiled by words.

In the Divine radiance, Nantu's darkened heart melted in ecstasy.

May God and the Enlightened Ones He has sent here to show us the way back home, Bless and Guide you always.

Michael

ABOUT THE AUTHOR

The author started his spiritual quest as a university freshman, after a long search for a true Master from an early age. Currently, and for the last 30 years he has been working as a volunteer at a spiritual retreat overseen by monastics, of which he was a coordinator for many years as well. The focus of the retreat is on meditation in an atmosphere of silence.

Michael is a partner in a Bio-Technology company doing Antibiotic and Anti-inflammatory research of which they have patented treatments. The company also sells over-the-counter health care products.

Swimming, roller skating, and tennis are his favorite sports. Rivers in New England are his number one choice for kayaking, and for long trips it was with a canoe accompanied by his trusty Samoyed traveling along as a guide.

You can contact him at:
bittersweetveil@gmail.com

I'm sure he would love to hear from you.

www.ingramcontent.com/pod-product-compliance
Lightning Source LLC
Chambersburg PA
CBHW071948150726
47999CB00001B/361